Fionuala, a goat of enquiring mind, i͟s
her ancestors, the Cool-Boys of Glen
dogged by the beautiful Siobhan, a Toggenburg ꭒꝉꝋꝳꝳ
Laragh, she sets forth on her odyssey, and naturally, being
Fionuala, finds adventure all along the way.

Cool-Boy House proves a disappointment; magnificent
stone goats on the gates and nary a one in the paddocks,
but she fulfills a lifelong ambition by riding in the *Tour de
Wicklow* which just happens to be passing by on Calary
Bog. At Roundwood she falls in with some very strange
people, finds that Moneystown isn't all it's cracked up to
be, and dreams of film stardom at Glendalough House in
Annamoe.

She meets Jacko, the Singing Donkey, alias the Laughing Jackass, who teachers her to dance and they decide to
audition for the circus as a song and dance act. Will Hurry
Harry put their names up in lights?

But she does — eventually — get to Glendalough. And
what a surprise she finds there ...

VERA PETTIGREW has lived for twenty-seven years in
Wicklow and knows every inch of the countryside through
which Fionuala wanders. This is her second book for The
Children's Press; her first was *The Adventures of Henry &
Sam & Mr. Fielding*.

TERRY MYLER's illustrations
are as brilliant as ever.

Vera Pettigrew

FIONUALA THE GLENDALOUGH GOAT

Illustrated by Terry Myler

THE CHILDREN'S PRESS

To
Cara, Niamh, Nooly, Kizz,
and all my animal friends

First published 1990 by
The Children's Press
45 Palmerston Road, Dublin 6

© Text Vera Pettigrew
© Illustrations The Children's Press

ISBN 0 947962 42 5 paperboards
ISBN 0 947962 43 3 paper

Typeset by Computertype Limited
Printed by Billing & Sons

This book is financially assisted by
The Arts Council/An Chomhairle Ealaíonn, Ireland

Contents

1

Sugarloaf Farm

Fionuala was bored. All the goats on Sugarloaf Farm had gone to the Goat Show, all except Fionuala. Once they took her to a show. They brushed her coat and trimmed her hooves, but she found the whole thing very stupid. At the show were many goats of all sizes and colours, some of them stuck-up creatures, not at all the type of goat that Fionuala liked.

'Walk round,' said the judge, and Fionuala walked and walked until she felt quite dizzy. Then the judge looked at each goat in turn, and when he came to Fionuala he said some rude things like 'knock-knees' and 'flat feet' and, worst of all, 'cow hocks'.

Fionuala couldn't believe her ears and looked everywhere for the cow before she realised he was talking about *her* legs. She didn't like that judge at all, and when she found his hat lying on the ground she ate the whole thing, right down to the lining. She ate a couple of rosettes too, which she hadn't won; very posh affairs, all red and shiny, and they tasted rather good. So all in all she had quite an enjoyable time, but they never took Fionuala to a show again.

So Fionuala dozed in her stall and chewed the cud and dreamed goat dreams, but you can't do that all day and after a while she began to feel bored. She put her two front feet on top of her half-door and looked out. The sun shone, the birds twittered and the grass looked green and inviting. A swallow flew by and then another, darting this way and that as they caught insects.

'Come out, Fionuala,' they called, 'come out into the sunshine,' but Fionuala couldn't go out because her door was bolted.

The farm cat came wandering along. He didn't like Fionuala for she often teased him, so he sat and washed right outside her door, and with a sly grin said, 'Too bad you can't come out, Fionuala,' and off he sauntered.

A little field-mouse scampered by. He ran in under the goat house door looking for oats, and out he ran again. 'Pity you can't get under the door, Fionuala,' he called as he went on his way.

By now Fionuala felt quite cross, so she pushed the door with all her might and, lo and behold, it opened and out she tumbled. She couldn't believe her luck as she lay there feeling quite dazed.

'Well, well,' she said to herself when her head stopped spinning, 'mustn't waste time. I want to enjoy myself,' and she staggered to her feet.

Round the corner she went and there, lying on a pile of straw, was the cat, fast asleep.

'I'll teach that cat,' thought Fionuala as she crept quietly up to him.

'Ba-a-a,' she shouted at the top of her voice, right in his ear.

The cat jumped three feet in the air with terror and dashed up a nearby tree, where he hid in the branches. Fionuala laughed and laughed until her sides ached.

'What's all that noise about?' said an angry voice,

and looking out of his house was Big Bill, the goat. He hadn't gone to the show either.

'What are you doing out of your shed?' he asked Fionuala crossly.

'Just having a little walkabout,' she answered.

'Who let you out?' asked Big Bill.

'I let myself out,' said Fionuala proudly, tossing her head.

'If you are such a clever goat, Nuala,' said Big Bill, 'perhaps you can let me out too.'

Now Fionuala didn't like Big Bill. He was a bossy fellow, and she hated being called Nuala, for wasn't she a direct descendant of the old warrior goat, Finbarr of Coolboy, who led his Herd into battle many times and always led them out victorious. So she said in her most haughty voice, 'I couldn't let you out. Your door is too high,' and off she ran before Big Bill could say another word.

Down the path she trotted, eating the odd nettle here and the odd dock there, until she came to the garden. Fionuala had never been in the garden but she had often looked in. It was a very pretty garden with roses and honeysuckle and a vegetable patch full of carrots. Now if there was one thing Fionuala loved it was a nice juicy carrot, so in she went and what a feast she had! Carrots, roses and honeysuckle all disappeared in a flash. She ate and ate until she couldn't eat any more.

'Now I think I'll have a little rest,' she thought and down she lay on a bed of lettuce and fell fast asleep in the warm sunshine. When she awoke the sun had gone and the rain was pattering down.

'I wonder where I can shelter?' she asked herself, and then she saw, standing on the lawn, a red umbrella. It was a very fine umbrella with pink roses painted all over it, and it was so big that Fionuala fitted completely underneath.

'This is nice,' she thought as she sniffed the pink roses. She didn't mean to eat those umbrella roses; it just happened. But once she started she couldn't stop, until all the roses were gone and there wasn't much of the umbrella left either.

'Oh dear,' she thought, 'that wasn't such a smart thing to do.'

She felt sorry for all the damage she had done, and she looked around to see if she could do anything to make amends.

'Those flower beds are very untidy,' she thought. 'I will do a little weeding.'

So Fionuala weeded and weeded, but as she didn't

know the difference between a flower and a weed, she pulled up everything until there wasn't a single thing left in the beds.

She was very careful to put everything in a neat pile beside the beds and she didn't eat one mouthful even though she would have loved a little snack, for she was trying hard to be a good goat.

'Well,' she thought at last, 'those beds look tidy now, but perhaps they are a little empty.'

Outside the back door stood a bucket of potatoes, all newly scrubbed and scraped. She didn't know that they were for the dinner and when she saw them standing there she thought, 'I will plant a nice bed of potatoes — that should please them.'

And plant them she did, row upon row of them, all neatly placed in the flower beds and well stamped

in. Then she hurried out of the garden.

As she passed the kitchen window, she caught sight
of her reflection in the glass and she stopped to have
a closer look. Inside the dogs were dozing. When they
saw Fionuala admiring herself they leaped at the
window with fierce barking. Fionuala liked dogs, but
they gave her such a fright that she made some rude
faces at them, and that made them bark louder than
ever.

'Stop your noise,' she called. 'Why are you shut in?
Wouldn't you rather be outside?'

'Of course we would,' said the dogs. 'We hate being
in here with nothing to do.'

'Perhaps I could let you out,' answered Fionuala,
as she did her best to open the kitchen window, but
she just couldn't manage it.

'Try the back door,' called the dogs. 'Surely you
can open that?'

So Fionuala obligingly went round to the back door.

'Bang, bang, bang,' shuddered the door as she hit
it with her head.

'Knock, knock, knock,' it thundered as she kicked
it with her feet.

It shivered and shook but it just would not open.

When Fionuala had finished kicking and banging the
door it looked a sorry sight.

'Goodness me,' she said to herself, 'I think I have
done a little damage,' and she looked in horror at the
lovely red door with the paint all scratched.

She turned into the stable yard and there, standing
against the wall, was a bicycle. It was a very old bicycle
and quite rusty, but if there was one thing that

Fionuala longed to do, it was to ride a bike. Many times she had seen her master cycle off to town, and she thought how grand it must be to whizz along the country lanes ringing the little bell. Fionuala had even had dreams in which she was riding a bicycle at top speed at the Goat Show, with everyone clapping and cheering. Then the judge would present her with not one but *six* rosettes for being the best rider at the Show.

Very carefully Fionuala wheeled the bicycle out from the wall. Then she stood and looked at it, for as she had only ridden a bike in her dreams, she didn't really know how to get on.

First she sat on the handlebars, and then she sat on the pedals, and when at last she managed to sit on the saddle, the whole bike fell over on top of her. But Fionuala was a persevering goat, and after many tries, and many falls, she managed to pedal slowly.

But she didn't want to ride slowly; she wanted to ride fast, as she did in her dreams. So she sat and thought about it, and then she had an idea.

At the far end of the stable yard was a grassy slope, and up this slope she pushed the bicycle. She was quite puffed when she reached the top, but at last she was ready. She jumped on the bike and accelerated down the slope. Across the yard she went, pedalling for dear life. Past the stables she streaked, round the corner, missing by inches Big Bill's shed and Big Bill himself who was looking out. Past the house and through the garden she flew — and straight into the duck pond.

One minute the ducks were swimming happily on the water; and the next minute a goat on a bike was swimming with them. With feathers flying and much

quacking, they left the pond. Flapping their wings and running and falling over themselves, they disappeared from sight.

Fionuala sat in the duck pond with water dripping from her head. Slowly she stood up. She felt one leg and then another, and another, and another, and to her amazement they were all there. She stepped out of the water and shook herself.

'That was some ride,' she thought and she began to feel very pleased with herself. 'I do believe I'll try it again.' But when she looked for the bicycle, she found to her horror it was all in bits. She took the broken parts, one by one, from the water and laid them on the grass — two wheels, a pair of handlebars, one saddle, and a little rusty bell. Fionuala looked at the poor bicycle, and she began to think that she hadn't been a very good goat.

'I must try to be better,' she told herself. 'Perhaps I could do something for the ducks, for I hope they don't die of fright.'

Lying beside the duck pond was a hose pipe.

'Those ducks could do with some water in their pond,' she thought. 'It is nearly empty and very muddy.' So she picked up the hose pipe, turned it on and filled the pond to overflowing. Then she made a little puddle for herself and what fun she had stamping in it and even rolling in it.

Nearby grew a lovely crop of dandelions and as she was very fond of dandelions she watered those too.

'That will make them grow well,' she said as she watered everything in sight, until at last the water stopped coming out of the hose pipe.

'I wonder what has happened to the water?' thought Fionuala who was really enjoying herself. She shook the hose pipe and looked up the nozzle, but not a drop of water could she see.

Now what Fionuala didn't know was that there was a water shortage and that it was a very bad thing to use so much water, and that the flow had stopped because there was no water left.

She went back into the stable yard and there, with head hanging over the stable door, was the brown mare.

'Where is your son?' asked Fionuala.

'Out in the field,' answered the brown mare.

'I'll go and have a little chat with him.'

'You leave him alone,' said the brown mare. 'I know your little chats,' but Fionuala was already on her way down the lane behind the stables.

'Hello there, Sonny,' she called over the gate.

Sonny was delighted to see her for he was feeling lonely all by himself.

'Come and play,' he whinnied. 'Let's have a race.'

Fionuala knew that Sonny got very excited when he galloped and that it was naughty to have a race, but with one skip and a jump she was over the gate and away she went as fast as she could, with Sonny racing after her.

Round and round they went, faster and faster, bucking and leaping, until Fionuala could run no more. But Sonny wouldn't stop. He was wild with excitement, and with a huge leap he jumped right over the wall into a field of cabbages.

Fionuala knew there would be trouble when Sonny was found in the cabbage field, so off she disappeared in the opposite direction.

Down in the meadow the bees were busy collecting

honey, and Fionuala stopped to watch them. She liked
the bees. She liked their soft furry coats and she liked
their humming; it made her feel sleepy.

'Dear gentle little bees,' she said as she dozed off,
but something was tickling her neck.

'Who did that?' she asked as she looked around, but
there was no one about, only the little bees. Again
Fionuala dozed, but this time the tickles went all down

her back and over her head too. Up she jumped in
alarm, to find bees crawling all over her.

'Stop,' she shouted, 'stop tickling me,' and she rolled
on the ground to get rid of the bees. Now if there
is one thing that bees don't like, it is shouting. They
buzzed angrily round Fionuala and tried to sting her.

'Help!' cried Fionuala and she began to run, past
the duck pond and the house and through the stable
yard, and she didn't stop running until she came to
the goat house. In she went and lay down on her own
bed, and as she had spent such a busy day she fell
fast asleep.

Just then the cows came into the yard on their way to be milked. A big black cow stopped by the goat house door to scratch, and it banged tight shut.

As the last rays of the sun disappeared in the sky, the farmer and his wife and all the goats arrived home from the Goat Show. What 'Ba-a-ing' and bustle there was as the goats settled down for the night!

When the cat in the tall tree saw the farmer and his wife, he set up a great wailing 'Mi-o-ow', the dogs in the kitchen started to bark, Big Bill rattled his stable door, and the ducks made a great quacking.

'What is wrong with the animals?' said the farmer. 'I have never heard them make such a din.'

'Look what is wrong with my garden!' cried his wife. 'All my flowers and carrots gone and my sun umbrella in shreds!'

'Who has done this?' shouted the farmer when he found the back door ruined and his bicycle in bits.

'Ask Fionuala,' shouted the animals. 'Fionuala did it,' but no matter how loud the animals shouted, the farmer and his wife, being only dumb humans, couldn't understand a single word they said.

2

Sugarloaf Mountain

At last all was silent on Sugarloaf Farm as the animals slept. The farmer and his wife stood in the darkness, looking into the goat house.

'I can't understand it,' said the farmer. 'Who could have done such damage while we were away?'

'I am sure it was Fionuala,' answered his wife. 'Only she could have been so destructive.'

'But she was locked in her shed,' said the farmer, and he scratched his head in puzzlement.

'Don't you remember what a wily old fellow her father was?' said his wife with a laugh. 'There was no door or gate over in Glendalough he couldn't open, and he ate everything within sight. Finn the Bin they called him.'

'I remember him all right,' said the farmer, 'and a rough old devil he was too,' and with a last look at the sleeping goats they went inside their house and shut the door.

Fionuala lay on her warm bed, and although her eyes were shut tight she was wide-awake and she heard every word the farmer and his wife said.

'Finn the Bin!' she said to herself indignantly. 'How dare they insult my father!' And to call him a rough old devil was unforgivable, for everyone in Ireland knew that her family were the Cool-Boys of Glendalough. Fionuala felt very angry indeed.

19

Then, suddenly, a thought came to her; a very exciting thought.

'I will go to Glendalough and look for my ancestors, for I have had enough of this lot here with their prize-winning and high and mighty ways,' and Fionuala trembled with excitement.

All night long she lay in the darkness and planned the journey, and when at last she did doze off she muttered and mumbled as in her sleep she travelled to Glendalough.

The first grey streaks of dawn were in the sky when she awoke. Not a sound was heard in the goat house except heavy breathing and snoring.

'Now to open the door,' she thought, 'but I must be very quiet or every goat in the place will be awake.' So first she pushed and then she shoved the door, but it didn't move an inch.

'Now what am I to do?' she wondered and she sat down to think.

'Well,' she said to herself at last, 'if my father could open any door, so can I!' And open it she did and it couldn't have been easier, for she just leaned over the top and slid back the bolt with her teeth.

She stood outside and breathed the damp dawn air. Behind the farm, wreathed in mist, rose Sugarloaf Mountain. If there was one thing that Fionuala had always wanted to do it was to climb that mountain, right to the very top.

On summer days as she grazed on its lower slopes, she often looked up and up to where the little clouds laughed as they drifted by in the blue sky, and she thought what a grand thing it would be to stand on

the very highest rock.

In winter Sugarloaf wore a white cap when the snow came falling softly, and sometimes gales came hurtling down the mountainside, rattling the doors and windows and making the goats frisk and jump in alarm. But when the rain came in great driving sheets they were glad to stay snug and warm in the goat house.

'I will climb Sugarloaf,' said Fionuala to herself, 'for surely that is the way to Glendalough.'

But before she could take even one step, a voice behind her said, 'Fionuala'. Fionuala's heart nearly stopped beating with fright. Slowly she turned round, expecting to see the farmer and his wife, but to her surprise she saw a young goat called Siobhan standing there. Now Siobhan was a very beautiful goat and had won many prizes at the Goat Show and even a silver cup, but she was the last goat Fionuala wanted to see as she was setting off for Glendalough, so she said in a cross voice, 'What do you want, for I am off on a journey and haven't time to hang about?'

'I hear you are going to Glendalough to visit your relations,' said Siobhan.

'And who told you that?' asked Fionuala nervously.

'I heard you talking in your sleep,' said Siobhan. 'Over and over again you said, "I am going to Glendalough to visit my family."'

'Can a goat not visit her family without the whole world knowing about it?' said Fionuala angrily, walking away.

'I think you are very brave to go out into the big wide world all by yourself,' said Siobhan, trotting after her. 'And I would like to come with you and visit my family too.'

'And who are your family may I ask?' said Fionuala, 'for I am not going all round Ireland looking for them.'

'I am a Toggenburg of Laragh,' said Siobhan proudly. 'My family came from Switzerland where we grazed the Alpine meadows, but for many years we have lived in Ireland.'

Fionuala stood and looked at Siobhan. She saw the soft brown and white coat and the dainty feet and slender legs, and she thought how grand it must be to come from Switzerland and be a Toggenburg from Laragh, but all she said was, 'I haven't the slightest idea where Laragh is, so you can't come with me,' and off she set at a great rate up the track to Sugarloaf.

'I know where Laragh is,' called Siobhan as she ran after Fionuala. 'It's on the way to Glendalough, so please may I come with you?'

'You really are a nuisance,' said Fionuala as up the path she panted. 'But if you don't talk too much, *and don't walk on my heels,*' she added, as one of Siobhan's tiny feet stepped on Fionuala's big one, 'you can tag along.'

The path up the mountain wound steeply, but the

goats could see only a few yards ahead, for a thick cold mist hung in the air. Clumps of gorse like pale ghosts with clutching fingers appeared and disappeared again, and when a sheep dashed out from behind a rock with its eerie cry echoing on the damp air, the goats got a great fright. Fionuala began to think of goblins and other strange creatures she had heard about. She stopped to look back at the farm but not a sign of it could she see and she began to wonder if they would be lost on Sugarloaf for ever.

'Is this the way to Glendalough?' asked Siobhan anxiously.

'Of course it is,' answered Fionuala, 'for we have to go up to go down.'

Suddenly the sky broke, the mist rolled back and the sun appeared. Now the goats were climbing through springy purple heather and green bracken. Overhead a kestrel hovered in the still air, and a raven, black as night, flew past with a loud 'cark, cark' as he went hunting. Little larks sang as they climbed and climbed in the blue sky.

Fionuala looked up and felt a quiver of excitement, for they were nearly at the top of the mountain. Now the two goats leaped and jumped over rocks and boulders, as surefooted as only goats are, until at last they stood on the very highest rock and looked around. Down below in the valley was the farm and they saw a man, like a tiny speck, coming out of the goat house.

'Probably out searching for us,' Fionuala thought, and she smiled at the shock the farmer would get when he found they were gone.

In the far distance was the sea, and as the goats

had never seen that before they gazed and gazed at
it in awe.

'Perhaps it is the Edge of the World,' said Siobhan
in a frightened voice, and the two goats turned away
to look in the opposite direction. Here stretched the
bog of Calary and beyond it the blue Wicklow
Mountains. Everywhere they saw something new and
wonderful — farms and houses, fields and rivers and
a road winding this way and that, with cars the size
of toys.

'Can we see Glendalough from here?' asked Siobhan,
and at that moment Fionuala saw the house. Even from
the top of the mountain it looked big, with turrets and
towers and beautiful gardens, and the more she looked
the more sure she became that she was looking at her
ancestral home. It was just as she had always imagined
it, and down the mountainside she ran, with Siobhan
running after her calling, 'Wait for me.'

But Fionuala wouldn't wait until she reached the
very bottom.

When she stopped running at last, her head spun
round and round and her breath came in short gasps
and she sat down in the heather with a bump.

When Siobhan finally caught up with her, she asked
peevishly, 'What happened to you? Why did you run
off like that and leave me behind? Did you see a ghost?'

'I saw my family home,' answered Fionuala. 'The
most beautiful house in Ireland, ancestral home of the
Cool-Boys of Glendalough, and I'm off now to visit
it,' and she stood up, fully recovered.

In her hurry she had run down the opposite side
of the mountain from the farm and now she had no

idea at all where she was, and to tell the truth she had no idea where Glendalough was either. A lane ran close by and into this she turned.

'Is this the way to your ancestral home?' asked Siobhan after a while.

'Of course it is,' answered Fionuala. 'It's just round a corner or two,' but no matter how many corners the goats went round they didn't find the house.

'This is very strange,' thought Fionuala, 'the house looked so close from the top of the mountain.' She began to feel a little foolish, with Siobhan asking all kinds of annoying questions like, 'Are you sure you know the way?'

And then she saw the signpost. One minute there was an empty country lane, and the next there was a signpost saying 'Glendalough 12 miles'.

'There you are!' cried Fionuala. 'I told you this was the

way!' And she stopped feeling foolish and felt very clever indeed, as off for Glendalough they set.

The road climbed steeply and above it the mountain top rose to a sharp point. There was a smell of honeysuckle and wild roses in the air, and a little rabbit sat on the grass verge washing his face. Fionuala would have liked to stop for a chat, but she was so anxious to reach her family home that she just hurried by.

Once or twice she looked back, and through the trees she thought she caught sight of the house, but the road seemed to be taking them in the opposite direction, which was strange indeed.

On they trudged until they came to a farmyard. Inside the farm gate a flock of geese sat sunning themselves. Fionuala and Siobhan stood and looked at them. After a while the father goose came waddling up. 'Be off with you,' he said to Fionuala. 'We don't want any goats here, and what are you staring at?'

'Not much,' said Fionuala who thought the father goose a very rude fellow. 'A goat can look at a goose.'

'Oh no she can't,' said the father goose hissing angrily. 'Off you go!'

'I don't like the look of this bad-tempered fellow,' said Fionuala. 'We had better be on our way.' And off she went with Siobhan running after her. When they had put a safe distance between them and the goose, Fionuala stopped and called out, 'BIG DUCKS', which is a very rude thing to say to a goose. Then she took to her heels up the Long Hill.

'Wait for me,' cried Siobhan, but Fionuala didn't stop until she reached the very top.

3

The Singing Donkey

Fionuala was really enjoying herself as she tripped along. She walked so fast that Siobhan could hardly keep up with her. Fionuala found her most annoying, for she talked non-stop.

'Wait for me,' bleated Siobhan.

'What's the hurry?' she cried.

'I'm tired!' she whined over and over again.

'Are you hard of hearing?' she asked finally.

'Of course not,' snapped Fionuala, 'my hearing is as sharp as a razor.'

'You don't seem to hear *anything* I say,' said Siobhan angrily.

'I hear what I want to hear,' answered Fionuala, and she walked on faster than ever.

The road wound this way and that and Fionuala kept a sharp look-out for the beautiful house she had seen from Sugarloaf Mountain, but there wasn't a sign of it anywhere.

'I hope I wasn't mistaken,' she thought. 'It surely was my ancestral home.'

The sun shone down and going round each corner was very exciting, for Fionuala never knew what she was going to see ahead, as Siobhan trailed far behind. For a long time she didn't see anything except tall hedges, until suddenly a voice, almost in her ear, said, 'Hello there, goat.'

Fionuala got a great fright, for she couldn't see anyone at all.

'Who's there?' she called nervously, and into her head came thoughts of bad malevolent fairies.

'I'm over here,' said the voice, 'on the other side of this hedge.'

Fionuala took a step nearer, and then another.

'Can't you see me?' said the voice. 'You must be very short-sighted.'

Fionuala didn't like being spoken to in such a fashion; it made her quite cross. And when she felt cross she stopped feeling afraid, so she marched right up to the hedge and peered through. She found herself looking at two very long ears.

'Good gracious me,' she said. 'Are you a rabbit?'

'Of course I'm not a rabbit,' answered the voice. 'I'm a donkey, and a famous one too.'

'Well,' said Fionuala, 'if you're famous why are you hiding behind that hedge?'

'Just you come in here and see for yourself,' said the donkey.

So through a gap in the hedge rushed Fionuala, with Siobhan running after her calling, 'Wait for me. Wait for me.'

Behind the hedge stood a large black donkey, with a rope round one of his front legs which was tied to one of his back legs.

'Why are you tied up like that?' asked Fionuala in horror.

'You may well ask,' said the donkey, 'but the truth is I'm hobbled.'

'What's hobbled?' asked Fionuala in alarm.

'Having my legs tied together like this so that I can't run away,' said the donkey. 'The old man who owns me is afraid I might go off and become famous again and then he wouldn't have me to work for him any more.'

Wiping away a tear or two, the donkey told Fionuala his story.

'Long ago, when I was young,' said the donkey, 'I belonged to a circus. Every night I went into the ring to sing and dance and pull a little cart full of boys and girls. I even had my name written up in lights — JACKO THE SINGING DONKEY. But one day my singing voice went away, and after a while I couldn't dance so well either. So the circus sold me to a man who wanted a strong donkey to pull a cart full of turf. Just imagine,' said the donkey, '... turf! Not boys and girls. Turf! So that is when I came here.'

'Well,' said Fionuala, 'perhaps I can help you. I'm very good at eating things. If you like I could chew off those ropes and then you could go and become famous again.'

'I'd like that very much,' said Jacko. 'And in return I could teach you to dance.'

So Fionuala chewed up all the ropes, and it didn't take long. Then she ate them, so that Jacko could never be hobbled again.

When he was free, Jacko taught Fionuala a little dance, a sort of jig, and round and round the field they danced until they were tired out. Then he sang a song but Fionuala thought he must indeed have lost his voice for it sounded most strange.

But Jacko seemed pleased with himself and said,

'You know, I think my voice is coming back.'

At last, when all the singing and dancing was over, Jacko noticed Siobhan for the first time. She had been standing in a corner of the field watching.

'Who is that?' he asked Fionuala. 'Is it your sister?'

'Certainly not!' answered Fionuala. 'She's a real pest of a goat who won't stop talking.'

Then she told Jacko that she was on her way to Glendalough to find her family and he listened with great interest.

'Where's that other goat going?' he asked.

'To Laragh,' answered Fionuala. 'She says she's a Toggenburg.'

'I know them well,' said Jacko, 'and a rich lot they are too.'

'Do you know the Cool-Boys of Glendalough?' asked Fionuala eagerly.

'I don't,' said Jacko, 'but then I'm not over that way often.'

As they talked, a shower of rain began to fall and Fionuala and Jacko joined Siobhan beside the hedge to shelter, but for once Siobhan said not a word; indeed she turned her back on Jacko.

'Don't you think we have been here long enough?' she whispered to Fionuala as the rain eased. 'I'm really surprised at the way you're hanging around here ... with that creature.'

'I'll stay as long as I want,' said Fionuala haughtily.

'Look!' said Jacko as the rain stopped and a beautiful rainbow appeared. 'If you find the end of that rainbow, you'll find the pot of gold!'

'Are you sure?' asked Fionuala.

'Oh yes,' said Jacko. 'Many's the farmer has become rich by finding it in his field.'

'Maybe we should have a look,' said Fionuala.

So round the field they tramped, and even Siobhan joined in. They searched in hedges and under stones, but all they found was a rusty old kettle full of beetles. When they looked again for the rainbow, it had faded and gone.

And so the time passed, and Fionuala and Jacko talked, and Siobhan, who couldn't keep quiet any longer, told of all the prizes she had won at all the

shows and of her family, the Toggenburgs of Laragh,
and Fionuala and Jacko grew weary listening to her.

'Well,' said Jacko at last, 'it's been nice meeting you
but I must be on my way.'

'Good luck,' said Fionuala, 'and I hope you become
famous again.'

'I hope you find your family,' said Jacko, as off he
trotted up the road.

Fionuala practised the little dance Jacko had taught
her, and after a while she too went off along the road,
dancing as she went, with Siobhan following her.

'Must you do that stupid dance?' asked Siobhan.
'It's most embarrassing watching you.'

'And what's stupid about it?' asked Fionuala angrily.
'And if you're so embarrassed, why don't you buzz
off and leave me alone,' and she danced harder than
ever.

'I really am getting good at this,' she thought.
'Perhaps I will become famous like Jacko.' She was
so busy thinking about being famous that she didn't
look where she was going, and she almost collided with
a big brown hare who was running across the road.

'Look where you're going,' snapped the hare crossly.
'And whatever do you think you are doing?'

'Dancing,' said Fionuala as she twirled round and
round.

'Dancing?' said the hare with scorn. 'Is that what
you call it? Wait until you see real dancing!' and he
began to leap in the air and stamp his big back feet.

Fionuala stood and watched the hare, and she had
to admit that he was a very good dancer indeed.

'Who taught you to dance like that?' she asked.

'All hares can do it. It just comes naturally.'

'Thump, thump, thump' went his big feet, and his leaps in the air got higher and higher, and he was very pleased to see how much he was impressing Fionuala.

'If you practise hard,' he said, 'you might become a good dancer, but never as good as a hare,' and off he ran like a streak of lightning.

'Must you talk to everyone you meet?' asked Siobhan. 'It's most unladylike.'

'I'll talk to whoever I like,' said Fionuala, 'and I'll dance whenever I like, and I'm really sick of you.'

'I'm not used to the type of creatures you associate with,' whined Siobhan as she flounced off in a huff, leaving Fionuala behind.

'That's got rid of *her*,' thought Fionuala. 'Perhaps I'll get a little peace now,' and she started to dance again. This time she tried to thump her feet on the ground like the hare had done, but her feet were quite small and no matter how hard she tried she couldn't make that 'thump, thump, thump'.

'Perhaps I should practise leaps in the air,' she thought. 'I'm sure I could do those.' So she leaped higher and higher, just like the hare had done, and faster and faster.

Now to dance like that is quite difficult when you have two legs, but when you have *four*, like Fionuala, it is almost impossible.

Suddenly, without any warning, her legs tied themselves into a tight knot, and when your legs are tied up in a tight knot, there is only one thing to do, and that is to fall right over.

'BANG!' went Fionuala, down on the hard road,

every ounce of breath knocked out of her.

As she lay there, she saw little stars floating round her head, and she began to think those pretty little stars were coloured lights saying — 'FIONUALA THE DANCING GOAT', and she smiled a happy smile as she floated off into a deep sleep.

Along the road came a farmer and his son with a flock of sheep. When the sheep saw Fionuala lying in the middle of the road all knocked out, they became very anxious and crowded round her crying 'ba-a-a-a' at the tops of their voices.

'Whatever is this?' said the farmer looking at Fionuala. 'A poor goat with her legs tied up in a knot. We can't leave her here.' And because he was a kind man, he and his son carried Fionuala into the sheep field and laid her down beside the hedge.

'We'd better get the knots of her legs,' said the farmer's son, and gently, one leg at a time, they unknotted Fionuala.

'I can't think how she got tangled up like that,' said the farmer. 'I have never seen such a thing before.'

'Anyway she looks quite happy,' said his son, for Fionuala still had a smile on her sleeping face.

'We will leave her here,' said the farmer, 'the sheep will look after her,' and he and his son went off.

After a time, through her sleep, Fionuala began to hear sounds, like a lot of goats talking. At first she thought she was back home in her own stable, so she opened her eyes and looked around. What a shock she got! For there were sheep everywhere; dozens and dozens of them.

'I must be dreaming,' she told herself and she closed

her eyes again, for she felt quite strange and dizzy. When she opened her eyes once more, a big sheep was standing looking at her.

'I'm glad to see you are awake,' said the sheep. 'We thought you were going to sleep for ever.'

Fionuala felt very foolish lying there, especially as she didn't know exactly how she had got there, so she said in a voice loud enough for all the sheep to hear, 'I wasn't really asleep, I just had my eyes closed.'

'You certainly were asleep,' said the big sheep. 'We found you in the middle of the road, with your legs tied up in a knot. The farmer and his son carried you here.'

Then Fionuala began to remember what had happened, and the more she remembered, the sillier she felt.

'I think I will have a little rest,' she said and closed her eyes again. But after a while she began to feel better, so she stood up and started to walk towards the gate.

'Don't go,' chorused the sheep. 'Stay for a chat.' But that was just what Fionuala didn't want to do.

'Thank you for your hospitality,' she said, 'but I must be on my way,' and off she set. But when she looked back all the sheep were following her, for sheep love to play follow the leader.

'Now what will I do?' wondered Fionuala. 'I can't take dozens of sheep with me everywhere.' So she stopped and ate a little grass, but every time she moved on, the sheep moved after her.

Then she had an idea. She knew that sheep are afraid of dogs, because dogs sometimes chase them, so at the top of her voice she shouted, 'DOGS'.

Off went the sheep at full speed over the hill and disappeared from sight. Fionuala laughed and laughed, but then she felt sorry for frightening them for they had been very nice to her.

She wandered this way and that, through field after field, not really knowing where she was going. Sometimes she jumped the banks, and sometimes she pushed through the hedges, and once she even ate her way through.

Just as she was wondering if she really was lost, a voice called, 'Fionuala', and there, looking over a gate, was Siobhan.

'Goodness me, she's back,' thought Fionuala. 'I'd forgotten all about her.'

'Where have you been?' she asked.

'Looking for you,' said Siobhan. 'I saw you lying on the road all tied up in knots — I just knew that dancing would do you no good.'

'Well thanks a lot for helping me,' said Fionuala.

'I couldn't help you,' answered Siobhan. 'Especially when you went off with those sheep — I don't like sheep.'

On the two goats wandered. Evening drew near and a thin pale sliver of a moon brightened the sky.

'Where will we sleep tonight?' asked Siobhan anxiously.

'We will find somewhere,' answered Fionuala, and sure enough they did, for in a corner of a field was a shed. Over the goats went, and it was a very nice shed with straw on the floor, and before you could wink they were both fast asleep.

4

Adventures on Calary Bog

Fionuala wakened with the dawn.

'Where am I?' she wondered with her eyes full of sleep, and then she remembered.

'This is the life for me,' she said to herself, 'I can go to bed when I like and get up when I like. No more being told by anyone what to do.' And she yawned happily.

Outside the shed was a large field, so big that it stretched away into the distance as far as the eye could see. Fionuala was admiring the landscape when suddenly she saw, just inside the hedge, a black bucket, and her nose told her there was something nice in that bucket, very nice indeed. Sure enough, it was full of lovely, crispy, crunchy oats, and if there was one thing that Fionuala loved, it was oats.

'What a feast,' she thought, and she began to gobble them as fast as she could.

'What are you eating?' asked a voice behind her as Siobhan appeared.

'Never you mind,' answered Fionuala rudely.

She was so busy munching and crunching that she didn't notice Siobhan disappearing fast, and she didn't hear galloping hooves until a loud voice shouted, 'STOP EATING MY OATS,' and there, getting nearer every second, was a huge black horse.

Across the field raced Fionuala with the horse

galloping after her. At the end was a gate, a very high gate, but she didn't hesitate. With one jump she was over it.

Now the horse could have jumped it too, but he was a hungry fellow and he wanted what was left of his breakfast. So he stopped chasing Fionuala and shouted some rude words after her. And she called some rude things back like 'broken-winded old nag' and 'knock-kneed gee-gee'.

When she had finished shouting insults at the horse, she found Siobhan beside her.

'Enjoy your breakfast?' asked Siobhan, but Fionuala didn't answer as she hurried along the road.

Calary Bog stretched on either side of the road, a great expanse of turf and heather. In the distance rose the blue Wicklow Mountains. A chill breeze blew over the flat bog land as great piles of dark clouds scudded by. Fionuala soon forgot her fright and as she walked she whistled a merry tune.

'Must you do that?' asked Siobhan.

'Do what?' said Fionuala.

'That awful whistling,' answered Siobhan. 'It quite makes my head ache.'

'You are nothing but a pain in the neck,' said Fionuala, and she whistled louder than ever.

After a while the goats came to a barn and beside the barn was a pigsty full of little piglets. Fionuala stood and watched them as they snuffled around and dug holes in the ground with their little snouts.

'What dear little creatures,' she thought, for she had never seen baby pigs before. 'What fun it would be to play with them.'

So she gave a hop and a skip, and jumped right into the middle of the sty. How the baby pigs squealed with delight and what fun they all had playing chasing games, and digging games, and rolling-on-your-back games! They were having such a good time they didn't notice Mother Pig arriving. She had been having a snooze when she was wakened by all the noise. When she saw Fionuala in the sty with her babies, she flew into a great rage and rushed at her, knocking her flying. Then Mother Pig kicked her with her feet, and hit her with her snout, and even tried to sit on her, and if Fionuala hadn't got up in the nick of time, she would have been squashed as flat as a pancake.

With one jump Fionuala was out of the sty and running up the road like the wind, and she didn't stop until she was a mile or two away, for of all the frights she had ever had that was the worst. As she ran she felt sure she heard Mother Pig coming after her, grunting and snorting, with her little eyes gleaming. But when at last she did dare to look behind, the road was quite empty.

She collapsed in a heap at the side of the road. A

big tree grew close by, with its branches nearly
touching the ground, and she crawled in under its
shelter. Now she felt safe, and as she was quite worn
out she fell asleep, and as she slept she dreamed a
dream.

It was night time in Fionuala's dream but as bright
as day, for a big yellow moon was shining. She was
walking beside a little tinkling stream. Moths flew here
and there, and bats went squeaking by.

Suddenly she heard the most beautiful music. It was
so beautiful that all the night creatures started to dance
and even the trees swayed to and fro as the air was
filled with its sweetness.

'Who is playing such wonderful music?' wondered
Fionuala, and then she saw him — a big pig dressed
in blue trousers and a red velvet waistcoat, sitting on
a tree trunk playing a little silver flute. He was a
handsome fellow, but she didn't like his little piggy
eyes. She was just about to creep quietly by, when
he called out, 'Hi there, goat, do you want to play
the flute?'

'Indeed I would like to, Sir,' she answered in a polite
voice for she felt afraid of him, 'but I don't know how.'

'It's easy,' answered the pig. 'All you have to do
is blow and it just plays itself. Catch!' and he threw
the little silver flute to Fionuala, and off he went and
disappeared from sight.

'What a lovely flute,' she said to herself. She put
it to her lips and immediately beautiful music poured
out, and once more all the trees and night creatures
started to dance. Fionuala felt very clever and she blew

and blew, and the flute played and played.

After a while she had no puff left, so she put the little flute down on the ground, but as soon as she did that it called out in an angry voice, 'Play me!'

Fionuala got the shock of her life, for she had never met a talking flute before. Then the flute jumped up and gave Fionuala a sharp tap on one of her legs. That hurt, so she quickly picked it up, put it to her lips and blew with all her might. Once more the beautiful music began. But if she stopped for even one second, the flute shouted, 'Play me' and gave her another sharp tap on her legs.

Soon she was quite worn out and her poor legs were black and blue. *Now* she knew why the pig had been so anxious to get rid of the magic flute, but when she tried to give it to some of the night creatures they all disappeared in a great hurry, calling out things like 'No, no, no!' and even 'Not on your life!'

Fionuala didn't know what to do and she began to feel quite weak from all that playing. Suddenly a cloud covered the moon and the silver world turned dark. Fionuala threw the flute with all her strength into the little tinkling stream, and off she ran as fast as she could.

'Come back,' screamed the flute as it scrambled out of the stream. 'Come back and play me.' But Fionuala ran on and on. Behind her ran the flute, faster and faster, nearer and nearer, and when Fionuala could run no more, and when the flute had nearly caught her, she woke up!

'What a terrible dream!' she thought as she lay under the chestnut tree with her heart going 'pit-a-pat'. 'How glad I am to have wakened up.'

Up above among the leaves a little wren sang a beautiful song and the air was filled with its sweetness.

'Tap, tap, tap!' went a branch of the tree, and at each tap it banged against Fionuala's legs.

'Well,' she thought after a time, 'I had better be on my way. If I stay here I might fall asleep again and I don't want that horrible dream to come back.'

So she peeped out from under the chestnut tree, just in case her dream might be true and the magic flute or the big pig were waiting for her, but there was no one in sight except Siobhan who was eating grass at the side of the road.

'So you're awake,' she said. 'Have you recovered from the beating that old pig gave you? I just knew no good would come of playing with baby pigs.'

'I'll play with whoever I like,' answered Fionuala as she crawled out from under the chestnut tree and started along the road again.

A warm sun shone down and she began to enjoy herself once more. Every so often she stopped for a snack, a blade of grass here and a leaf or two there, until they came to an avenue with iron gates standing wide open. On either side of the gate were large pillars, and on top of each pillar was a beautiful stone goat.

Fionuala stood and looked at those stone goats, and then she saw something else. For the name on the gate, written in lovely gold lettering, was Cool-Boy House.

'Look at that!' she said to Siobhan excitedly. 'I do believe my family live here,' and in through the gates with her and up the avenue.

'I thought your family lived at Glendalough,' called Siobhan as she ran after her.

'And so they do,' answered Fionuala.

'This isn't Glendalough,' said Siobhan, but Fionuala wasn't listening, for she had just caught sight of the house. It was a very big house surrounded by green lawns, and standing in the middle of one of the lawns was a large tent. Fionuala just had to see what was in that tent, so she walked right up to it and looked inside. She couldn't believe her eyes, for all round the tent were coloured lights which twinkled and shone.

'Goodness me,' she said to herself, 'this must be a circus. Perhaps Jacko is here and is going to have his name written up with these little lights,' and at the top of her voice she called, 'Jacko, where are you?'

The words were no sooner out of her mouth than there was a deep growl, and into the tent walked a large dog, with his lips drawn back in a nasty snarl showing a mouthful of yellow teeth. As you know, Fionuala liked dogs, but she didn't like that dog.

She acted quickly. She rushed at him and when she almost reached him, she jumped right over his head and shot out of the tent like a jet plane. In front of her was the house, with a flight of steps leading up to the open front door. Up the steps she flew and right through the front door. At any moment she expected to hear the dog snapping at her heels, but when she looked back he was standing at the bottom step, for a long chain tied to his collar had stopped him.

Fionuala closed her eyes so that she couldn't see him, and when she opened them again he had disappeared. Of Siobhan there was not a sign.

Fionuala had never been in a house before and when she got her breath back she looked around her. She was standing in a large entrance hall with many pictures on the walls and in one corner hung a pair of goat's horns. Fionuala didn't like the look of those horns one bit, and if it hadn't been for the awful dog outside she would have run straight out of the front door again. Trying not to look at the horns she began to explore.

There were many rooms leading from the hall and Fionuala looked into each one. Some were quite small and she passed them by with only a glance, until she came to a very large room. As she peered in, she saw sofas and chairs with cushions, and little tables with bowls of flowers. A soft carpet covered the floor, the very colour of the sun, which streamed in through four long windows, nearly blinding her with its golden light.

Now Fionuala had never sat in a chair, so she tried each one in turn. Then she tried the sofas and she

even put her feet up to rest for a minute or two.

After a while she began to smell a delicious smell. She sniffed and then sniffed again, and she followed the smell across the room and through a door, and what a sight met her eyes! In the middle of another large room stood a table simply groaning with food. There were plates and dishes piled high with cakes and sandwiches and sausage rolls and jellies and trifles and meringues and turkey and ham and everything you could think of, and in the centre of it all was a beautiful wedding cake.

Fionuala had never been to a wedding, and she had never seen such a feast before, and the sight of all that food, with no one there to eat it, was too much for her. Round the table she went, having a taste of this and a lick of that, and she even tried the beautiful wedding cake. She looked out of the windows to see if any of her family, the Cool-Boys of Glendalough, were grazing in the large paddocks outside, but there wasn't a goat in sight.

'Perhaps they don't live here any more,' she thought in disappointment.

Now feeling a little sleepy, she went back to the entrance hall.

'I wonder what is up there?' she thought as she looked up the wide staircase, and up the stairs she trotted. There were many rooms upstairs, but the first one was so inviting, with a nice soft bed, that she just lay down on it and went fast asleep.

She didn't know how long she had been asleep when suddenly she was wakened by the sound of voices in the hall and the sound of laughter on the stairs. Off the bed she leaped and out on to the landing she ran, but it was too late! The stairs were full of ladies in large hats, all coming towards her. The only way down was by the banisters and that was the way she went.

One minute she was on the landing; the next she was flying down the banisters past all the astonished ladies. What pandemonium there was then with everyone shouting and fainting, but she didn't stop and out through the front door she galloped like an express train.

At that very moment the bride and groom were coming up the steps. As Fionuala swept past them the bride gave a scream; her bouquet of flowers flew out

of her hand and landed right on top of Fionuala's head, and there it stayed as she streaked across the lawn, back down the avenue and out through the open iron gates.

After a while she stopped running and as she wandered along the road in the warm sunshine a cyclist sped by, going at a great rate, and then another, and another. Fionuala watched as dozens more flew past, and suddenly in the distance she heard shouting and cheering.

'I do believe it's a race,' she thought and her eyes danced with excitement, for, as you know, Fionuala was a great cyclist.

'How I wish I could join in,' she thought. 'If only I had a bike.'

At that moment, as if her wish was being granted,

her eyes fell upon a bicycle. It was a lovely bicycle, all red and shiny. In fact it looked quite new, and there it was, lying at the side of the road all by itself as if it didn't belong to anyone.

Fionuala didn't waste a minute. As another batch of cyclists appeared she jumped on the bike and joined them. Zooming round corners and up and down hills they went, and Fionuala with them, cycling for dear life. She bent low over the handlebars just as the other cyclists were doing, with the wind whistling past.

As she stole a glance sideways now and then, she noticed that all the cyclists wore nice little caps.

'I would like one of those,' she said to herself, but then she remembered she was wearing the beautiful bridal bouquet of flowers. In fact she could even see some of the little flowers bobbing up and down on her forehead as she cycled, and she felt a very well-dressed goat.

On and on they went, and then a strange thing happened. The cyclist next to Fionuala turned his head and looked at her. As their eyes met he gave a strange cry, almost a scream, and suddenly his bike disappeared from under him and he was left lying flat on the hard ground.

'I wonder what happened to him?' thought Fionuala, and she cycled on harder than ever. A few minutes later the same thing happened with another cyclist, and then another, and another. The moment they looked at her their bikes just seemed to fall from under them. She couldn't understand it at all, for she had given each one a very nice smile.

Soon there weren't many cyclists left in the race,

and finally none at all, as they had all fallen by the wayside. Ahead was the finishing line and Fionuala could hear the crowd shouting, 'Come on, Stephen.' Then to her amazement she heard them calling *her* name too. It wasn't exactly her name, but she knew they meant her.

'Come on, kid,' roared the crowd.

Now Fionuala wasn't a kid. In fact she hadn't been a kid for a long time, but she knew she was a young-looking goat who didn't show her age at all.

As the crowd roared again Fionuala made her fatal mistake! She looked behind — just in case there *might* have been another goat in the race — and that was her undoing.

One moment she was heading for the finishing line. The next, she was flying through space, over the heads of the spectators and the cars and even over the TV cameras. It seemed to take her a long time, and she

saw all the surprised faces looking up at her until, at
last, down she came, right in the middle of Calary Bog.
As she lay there, she heard the voices and the shouting
dying away in the distance, but of her lovely red bike
there was not a sign.

She lay on the bog looking at the blue sky above
and listening to the larks singing. Presently she heard
the sound of a gurgling stream and she realised how
thirsty she was. She stood up and looked around. All
was peace and quiet, with the bog stretching away into
the distance. Clumps of heather and gorse grew
everywhere and the air was filled with the soft buzzing
of many insects and the distant murmur of water.

She picked her way over the turf until she came
to a little tumbling stream which rushed over and
around the stones, flinging drops of water high into
the air. Bending low over the river bank, she stretched
her neck as far as she could until her lips touched the
ice-cold water, and she drank and drank. Then she
sat on the bank and dabbled her hot tired feet in the
cool greenness.

After a while she strolled along the grass at the
water's edge. The stream wound this way and that,
with little gushing waterfalls and still dark pools, and
at one of these pools Fionuala stopped. As she leaned
over the water she saw her reflection dancing on the
surface, and on her head the flowers of her bouquet
glowed with colour.

'How beautiful they are,' she said to herself. 'How
glad I am that I didn't lose them in that cycle race,'
and she turned her head this way and that admiring
herself. Then she leaned over just that bit too far, and

before she could save herself she fell with a splash into
the water. Spluttering and coughing she climbed out
of the pool, dripping wet, just in time to see her
beautiful flower head-dress being carried away by the
swift flowing water, on and on and out of sight.

How upset she was! But being a happy goat by
nature, she soon began to enjoy herself again. Little
fish darted through the water and Fionuala watched
them for a long time. She loved to see the flash of
silver, as twisting and turning they went on their way.

She was so busy watching them that she nearly
didn't see the basket. It was lying on the river bank
and it was a very unusual basket, not at all the kind
you take shopping. It was quite big with a lid which
fastened with two leather straps and Fionuala just had
to undo those straps and open it.

Inside on a bed of damp grass lay six beautiful fish,
but they didn't look very happy. In fact they looked
most uncomfortable, for their sides heaved and their

mouths opened and closed, as they gasped for air.
Fionuala was quite shocked.

'You poor little creatures,' she said. 'Who has taken
you out of your lovely stream and put you into this
horrible basket?'

She picked up the basket and emptied the fish back
into the water. How pleased those fish were, and as
the water closed over them, with a splash of joy they
were gone.

'Well,' she thought, 'I may as well make use of this
strange basket, for it would make a very nice seat.'

Now Fionuala was a rather heavy goat and the basket
wasn't meant for sitting on, so there was a dreadful,
cracking, splintering noise as she squashed it flat.

At that moment two fishermen came round a bend
in the river bank carrying their rods. To their horror
they saw a large goat sitting on their fishing basket
which was now quite squashed. But, worst of all, their
fish were gone.

With cries of rage they ran at Fionuala and began
to beat her with their rods. She hadn't seen them
coming — in fact she had been admiring the scenery
— and she got a great shock when they began to hit
her. She leaped up in panic and began to run, but
she missed her footing and once more she landed right
in the middle of the stream. Water flew everywhere,
soaking the fishermen, while Fionuala, gasping and
choking, was making for the far bank. Once on dry
land, she took to her heels.

'I must really learn to swim,' she thought, 'for the
water was quite pleasant.'

5

Roundwood

As Fionuala came near Roundwood the sky grew black. Big clouds rolled up and in the distance thunder rumbled. She had been in a thunderstorm once. She and all the goats on Sugarloaf Farm were grazing in the fields when large hailstones beat down on them, the thunder clapped and great flashes of lightning lit up the sky. The goats had run here and there, calling for the farmer and when he came for them they rushed in panic through the farm and into the goat house.

Now as Fionuala trotted along the road to Roundwood, the thunder rolled again, closer and closer.

'Where will I go?' she thought in panic.

At that moment she came to a school, and into the playground she hurried and right up to the school door. She gave the door a push and to her great relief it opened, and as the first drops of rain began to fall she ran inside and closed the door behind her.

Fionuala had never been in a school before, so she looked at the desks, and the blackboard, and the pictures on the walls, and all the books. She smelt the chalk, and the markers, and the plants on the window sill, and she thought it was quite the nicest place she had ever been in. She sat on the teacher's chair, and she looked out of the window. She saw the lightning flash, and she listened to the rain beating on the roof and she felt warm and safe.

Suddenly she heard footsteps. She froze, still as a statue, and her heart went 'pit-a-pat, pit-a-pat' as someone walked through the playground and right up to the schoolroom door. Then the key turned in the lock, and the footsteps died away. Fionuala was locked in! But she didn't mind one bit. She had another look around the class-room, examining this and that.

In a corner stood a cupboard full of books. Fionuala looked at each one. There were books about pigs and dogs and cows and horses and a very nice one called *The Adventures of Henry & Sam & Mr. Fielding* and she liked it so much that she read it through from beginning to end. Twice! But although she looked everywhere, there wasn't even one book about a goat.

'How disappointing,' she thought.

At last the thunder and lightning stopped. Darkness crept into the schoolroom, and Fionuala couldn't read any more. At the end of the room were two doors, one painted blue, and one painted pink. On the pink door there was a drawing like this and on the blue door a drawing like this:

Fionuala opened the second door and looked inside. She saw a tiny room with a wash-hand-basin and a little seat with a wooden top, but it was quite a cosy room, and she went inside and fell asleep at once.

She slept so deeply she didn't notice the morning coming, and she didn't hear the birds singing, and she didn't hear the children arriving, until the door opened and a little boy came in.

Fionuala wakened with a start, and she looked at

the little boy and he looked at her in amazement.

Finally, remembering her manners, she said, 'Good morning.'

'Good morning,' said the boy. 'What are you doing here?'

So Fionuala told him how she was on her way to Glendalough to find her family, and they talked so much that the teacher called out, 'What are you doing in there, Seán? Are you ill?'

'No, Miss,' answered Seán as he came back into the class-room, 'I'm quite well, thank you. I was just talking to the goat in the toilet.'

Then all the children ran to see the goat and there were so many of them they crowded the doorway, so Séan led Fionuala into the class-room. Then Miss Right, who was a very nice teacher, invited Fionuala to sit in the front desk and to tell them about a goat's life.

So she told them all about Sugarloaf Farm and how she was travelling to Glendalough to find her family. She even told them about the awful judge at the Goat Show, and they laughed and laughed when they heard how she had eaten his hat right down to the lining. Then she listened while the children did their lessons, and being a very clever goat she knew the answers to many of the questions Miss Right asked.

So the morning wore on. All the children drew lovely pictures of Fionuala and she felt a very important goat indeed. Then they shared their lunch with her, and she had a very happy time. Now the sun was shining and Fionuala whispered to Seán, 'I must leave,' and when no one was looking she slipped away.

'I *must* write a book about a goat,' she told herself,
as she hurried along the road. And so she came to
Roundwood.

Fionuala had never been in a village before and she
stood in the shadow of a wall and watched. There was
bustle and noise everywhere, with people coming and
going, and cars and even a tractor or two. There were
shops with exciting things in the windows, and one
beautiful shop had so many kinds of fruit and
vegetables that Fionuala's mouth began to water.

Then she heard two men on the other side of the
wall talking, and she heard every word they said —
or she *thought* she did.

'Hello there, Pat,' said the first man. 'Any chance
of a few oats?'

'Well now,' said Pat, 'I'll see if I can find you some.'

'If you do, could you put them in a sack and drop them round to my place?' asked the first man.

'I will for sure,' said Pat. 'I'll go and look for them now.'

Fionuala's blood froze in her veins, for she thought the men were talking about *goats*, not oats!

'I must get away from here,' she thought in terror. 'If those men see me they'll put me in a sack,' and she looked around wildly for somewhere to hide. Nearby was an open window and in through it she dashed like lightning — and only in time — as the two men passed by.

She found herself in a large hall with rows and rows of chairs and a platform at one end. She knew there must be another way out, but just as she spotted it the door opened and a stream of people poured in and began to sit on the chairs. The hall was dimly lit, and before anyone noticed her Fionuala ran to the back row and sat down close to the wall.

'Those men will surely find me,' she thought. 'What am I to do?'

Then she saw a straw hat and sun-glasses lying on a seat beside her and, quick as a flash, she grabbed them up and put them on. At that moment a large lady in a fur coat pushed her way along the row of chairs and sat down beside her; she was so large she nearly sat *on* Fionuala. Behind her came a little man in a bright check shirt. It took them quite a while to settle themselves and they talked loudly all the time.

Suddenly Fionuala realised in dismay that the large lady was talking to her.

'I see you are wearing your fur coat too, honey,' she drawled. 'I always say a fur coat is the only thing to wear in little old Ireland,' and she laughed noisily.

Fionuala didn't like being called 'honey', and she didn't much like that loud-mouthed person either, so she looked the other way and pretended she hadn't heard a word.

'Pardon me,' said the woman, digging Fionuala in the ribs with her elbow, 'but is your coat ponyskin?'

At that, Fionuala felt very enraged, and she said at the top of her voice, 'GOAT'. In fact she said it so loudly that people turned to stare at her.

'Well, what-do-you-know,' said the woman to her husband, 'this lady is wearing a GEN-U-INE Irish goatskin coat. That's real cute, I'd sure like one myself,' and she turned to Fionuala and began to talk non-stop.

'Are you local?' she asked after a while.

'From Glendalough,' answered Fionuala.

'Do you hear that, Ed,' the woman yelled at her husband. 'This lady comes from Glendalough, and that's where we're going to look for our ancestors.'

'My family are the Cool-Boys,' said Fionuala proudly.

'Wow,' said the fat lady, 'that must be a real old family. Are they rich?'

'Very,' answered Fionuala.

At that moment a man walked quickly on to the platform. 'Good afternoon, ladies and gentlemen,' he said, 'we are about to start our cookery class.'

'Cookery,' screamed the fat woman. 'I though you said it was a Poetry Reading. Ed, let's get out of here

and find some culture,' and they left the hall, causing a great disturbance.

Fionuala tried to leave too, but the man on the platform fixed her with such an angry look that she sat down again quickly.

Soon she began to feel drowsy, what with the heat and the crowd and the straw hat and the sun-glasses she was wearing. As the cookery class droned on and on, she nodded into sleep.

Suddenly she wakened and sat bolt upright in her chair.

'Take two kidneys,' said the man, 'and chop them into little pieces.'

Now, as you know, Fionuala didn't always hear

clearly, and she was quite sure the man said, 'Take two *kids* and chop them into little pieces.'

With a yell that nearly lifted the roof, she made for the door. Off flew her straw hat and sun-glasses. She overturned chairs and the people sitting on them.

'Catch that goat,' someone shouted, but Fionuala was too quick for them. Though the door she shot and down the corridor at top speed. Ahead was another door. She crashed in like a thunderbolt, and that was when she got the shock of her life — for the room was full of goats. Well, at first glance the room was full of goats, but it took her only a second to see that they weren't goats at all, but people dressed as goats!

There were fat people and tall people, thin people and short people, all wearing goat costumes. At one end of the room was a band, and they too were dressed as goats. Fionuala stared in disbelief. 'I must leave this place,' she thought and she turned for the door, but before she knew what was happening, she found herself pulled into a long line as the band started to play.

'Sing,' shouted a tall man in a white shirt, and everyone began to sing at the tops of their voices while they shuffled around as if they were doing the Conga. The song went on and on and at the end of each verse they shouted, 'WE ARE THE GOATS'. Fionuala had never seen or heard anything so ridiculous in her entire life.

Just when she thought she couldn't stand it for another moment the band stopped playing and the tall man approached her.

'You're not much of a singer,' he said, 'but your goat costume is superb. Come to the head of the line. Lead the dance.'

'It's not fair,' whined a girl beside Fionuala, 'Why should she have a better costume than the rest of us?'

'Stop complaining,' snapped the man angrily. 'Wear the costume you're given or get out of the show.'

When they started dancing again, the girl gave Fionuala a few sly kicks. However, Fionuala, who was very good at butting, managed to give her a few quiet butts when no one was looking.

'Will I ever get away?' she thought in despair.

At long last, after much more singing, the man in the white shirt held up his hand. 'That will do for today,' he said. 'You can take off your costumes now.'

'What am I to do?' thought Fionuala, but in the pushing and shoving that followed, she managed to slip quietly out of the hall. Keeping close to the houses she walked quickly down the deserted village street and out into the countryside again.

6

Annamoe

Fionuala was glad when she had left the village of Roundwood behind. 'Glendalough 7 miles' said the signpost and her step quickened. She was so deep in thought she didn't hear a voice calling 'Fionuala', and up behind her, panting hard, ran Siobhan.

'Where have *you* come from?' asked Fionuala. 'I thought you must have gone back to Sugarloaf Farm.'

'I've been searching for you *everywhere*,' complained Siobhan. 'I think you are very mean to have forgotten about me.'

'I didn't forget about you,' said Fionuala. 'You just disappeared at Cool-Boy House.'

'When I saw that awful dog I hid in the bushes,' said Siobhan. 'Then when you came out at last, you raced right past me ... and I have been looking for you ever since.'

On the two goats walked in silence, for Siobhan was sulking and Fionuala wasn't at all pleased to see her again. Now the road followed a fast-flowing river where herons flapped lazily over the water. They passed a hill covered with gorse, and its perfume filled the air as they came to the little village of Annamoe.

At the bend in the road was a beautiful cottage with a lovely straw roof. There was a garden full of flowers and on the lawn stood a table laid for tea. It was all so peaceful and inviting that Fionuala stopped to look.

'Armstrong's Barn' said the sign on the gate.

'What a strange name,' she said to Siobhan. 'I wonder who Armstrong is, and I don't see his barn anywhere.'

At that moment two little children ran out on the lawn, laughing and playing, and Fionuala lent over the gate to watch. They were having such a good time they didn't notice her until she sneezed.

'A-tish-oo,' she went, not once but over and over again.

'Oh, look at the goat,' shouted Rocco, the little boy, and he and his sister Isabella ran to the gate.

At that moment a lady came out of the cottage carrying a tray full of all kinds of good things — chocolate biscuits, and coffee cake, and ice cream and lots more. When she saw the goats she gave a cry of alarm.

'Chase them away,' she called, 'for they will destroy our garden and eat the roof off our house.'

'They were very nice goats,' said the children sadly as Fionuala and Siobhan disappeared along the road.

'Well what do you think of that?' said Siobhan indignantly. 'I'm sure we wouldn't have been treated in that way if they knew I was a Toggenburg of Laragh.'

They came to a bridge and they stopped to watch the water flowing fast underneath, swirling over the rocks and stones. They passed pretty white cottages with gardens full of roses and Fionuala stopped to smell their perfume, but she didn't eat a single petal for it would have been a shame to spoil those lovely gardens.

She was so busy admiring the flowers that she didn't

notice a little goat looking over a wall until he called
out, 'Hi there, Missus.'

He gave Fionuala quite a shock and she felt angry.
But when she saw that he was very young and a nice
little fellow, over she trotted for a chat. They talked
of this and that and Fionuala asked him to do a few
sums in his head, and he was so good at it that he
had the answers even before she had. Siobhan didn't
say a word, for she wasn't at all good at sums, and
after a while she grew bored.

'Are you coming or are you not?' she said to
Fionuala. 'I'll never find my family at this rate.'

'Where do your family live?' asked the little goat.

'They are the Toggenburgs of Laragh,' answered
Siobhan haughtily.

'I'm an Anglo-Nubian myself,' said the little goat. 'My family came from Europe and the Far East. We look different from other goats because of our long ears.'

'You are a handsome little fellow,' said Fionuala as she looked at his soft mottled coat and big droopy ears. 'My family are the Cool-Boys of Glendalough. Do you know them?'

'I don't think so,' said the little goat, 'but there is a house here in the village called Glendalough Lodge.'

'A big house?' asked Fionuala.

'A *very* big house,' said the little goat.

'Can you direct me there?' asked Fionuala.

'It's just down there by the bridge,' said the little goat. 'First turn on the right, up a long avenue.'

'Do any goats live there?' asked Fionuala.

'I don't know about goats,' he answered, 'but there are plenty of wild animals.'

'Wild animals?' said Fionuala. 'What wild animals?'

'All kinds,' said the little goat. 'Roaming the woods and the fields.'

'Don't talk such nonsense,' said Fionuala crossly. 'There are no wild animals in Ireland. What would your mother say if she heard you telling such tales?'

At that moment a man came out of a nearby shed.

'Who is that?' asked Fionuala.

'That's Pat,' answered the little goat. 'He's my owner.'

Then Fionuala remembered the man called Pat in Roundwood, and she thought with horror of goats being put in sacks, and off she ran as fast as she could, leaving the little goat staring after her in astonishment.

Down the road she rushed, with Siobhan running after
her, until she came to the bridge, then along by the
river to a wooden gate, and there she stopped.

'What happened?' asked Siobhan when she caught
up with her. 'Why did you run off like that?'

'It wasn't safe to stay there,' answered Fionuala
darkly.

'Glendalough Lodge' said the sign on the gate, which
she opened and closed carefully, for if her family did
live there, she didn't want them to run away before
she had even met them. Along the avenue she and
Siobhan strolled.

'I can't understand that little goat telling such
naughty stories,' said Fionuala. 'Wild animals indeed!
I don't know what kids are coming to nowadays.'

The avenue wound through rolling green fields, and
the sound of the river was close by. Tall trees grew
everywhere. On the two goats went until they came
to a very strange tree. It had dark spiky leaves, sharp
as needles.

'That's a Monkey Puzzle,' said Fionuala. 'It's the
only tree a monkey can't climb.'

'If that's so,' said Siobhan, 'why is there a monkey
sitting in this one?' and she pointed high up above
her head.

'Don't be ridiculous,' said Fionuala. But as she
stared up amongst the prickly branches she gave a gasp,
for there *was* indeed a monkey.

At that moment Siobhan gave a loud cry as she sank
to her knees in the grass.

'Look,' she whispered, and as Fionuala followed her
gaze she too grew weak, for standing a few feet away

looking at them was a lion!

As she waited for it to spring, the blood pounded in her ears and she could almost feel his terrible teeth. But nothing happened. The seconds turned to minutes, and still the lion didn't move.

At that moment a red squirrel appeared, collecting nuts. When he saw Fionuala and Siobhan frozen to the spot, he began to shake with laughter.

'I see the lion has you fooled,' he said. 'You both look as if you are about to die of fright. But he's not real, you know.'

'What do you mean?' asked Fionuala.

'Just that,' said the squirrel. 'He's a fake!'

'What's he doing here then?' asked Siobhan.

'He belongs to the film company,' said the squirrel. 'He's one of their props. There's a monkey in that tree there, and a crocodile down by the river, and a snake and lots of others, all fakes. They're making a film here.'

Fionuala felt very silly then, but for once she couldn't think of anything to say for her brain was numb with fear. When she found her voice she asked, 'Are there any goats here ... I mean real goats?'

'Not that I know of,' said the squirrel, suddenly disappearing up a tree.

'I would love to be a film star,' said Siobhan. 'I feel there is acting in my blood.'

'You wouldn't have a drop of blood left in your body if that lion had been real,' said Fionuala tartly.

On the goats wandered and soon they saw the fake crocodile by the river and the fake snake in the tall grass, and they looked very real indeed.

'But look at that,' said Fionuala, pointing. 'That's
a bit of a mess! Nobody could think that was a bull,
for he doesn't look a bit real, does he?' and she sat
down on the reclining figure.

'Siobhan,' she called, 'this is fun,' as she bounced
up and down, but of Siobhan there was no sign.

It took her only a moment or two to realise that
there was a very strange sound coming from beneath
her, and it wasn't a very nice sound at all. The bull
stood slowly up and Fionuala went tumbling into the
long grass, for he was *real*!

He stood looking down at her and she cowered into
the grass as she saw the huge body, and the small eyes,
and the nose with a ring in it. Then she realised that
the bull was laughing!

'Didn't that give you the great fright?' he said, 'but
get up. I won't hurt you, for I would be glad of a
bit of company.'

So Fionuala and the bull talked of all kinds of things,
and Siobhan came creeping out from behind a tree
where she had hidden, and the bull told them all about
films, and the goats were most impressed for they had
never met a film star before.

After a while, when the bull stopped speaking, they
heard voices and a noise that sounded like 'plink-plonk'
over and over again.

'What's that noise?' asked Fionuala.

'The people up at the house are having a tennis
party,' explained the bull. 'You should go and watch,
it's good fun. I'll just stay here and have a snooze.'

So the two goats walked on until they saw the house.
It was indeed a large house with many windows and

virginia creeper covering its grey walls. There were lawns and flowers and trees and the tennis court, where people dressed in white were running here and there chasing a little ball.

'Plink-plonk' went the little white ball, as it flew backwards and forwards over the net, as the people hit it with all their might with their tennis racquets.

Fionuala and Siobhan stood under a tree watching. Suddenly, without warning, the ball came flying straight at Fionuala. Without a second's hesitation she caught it and threw it back, just as a girl appeared around the corner of the house carrying a tray of cool drinks.

Unfortunately Fionuala wasn't a very good shot, and she sent the ball whizzing through the air in the wrong direction. It landed right in the middle of the tray of drinks. Up flew the tray in the air, and down went the glasses to the ground with a great crash.

Everyone was running and shouting, and before they knew what was happening Fionuala and Siobhan were caught. But instead of being cross with them, everyone made a great fuss of them and gave them nice things to eat, like iced buns and cheese-cake and even chocolate.

'These goats are just what we want,' said a young lady. 'They will be perfect for the film.'

Fionuala and Siobhan couldn't believe their luck as they were patted and fussed over.

'We will put them in one of the stables for the night,' said the young lady. 'There is plenty of room, for the horses are all out, and tomorrow we will film them.'

Fionuala and Siobhan had never seen such beautiful stables before. On the doors were names such as 'Painted Lady' and 'Swallow Tail' and 'Red Admiral' and a strange one which said 'Cabbage White'. Inside, the floors were covered with straw as deep as a mattress. There was fresh water and sweet meadow hay, oats and apples and even a pear or two.

When the goats had eaten all they could, and even more, they were glad to rest in such luxury. As it grew dark the lights in the house came on and there was the sound of music and laughter, for a party was starting. Cars came and went and the smell of food wafted out from the kitchens.

'I think I will take a walk,' said Fionuala, for she loved a party.

'I will stay here,' said Siobhan, biting into a juicy red apple. 'I must get my beauty sleep.'

'Vain creature,' thought Fionuala as she opened the stable door and slipped outside.

'Mind you don't get fat,' she called as she hurried off.

Fionuala spent a long time watching through the lighted window. Couples whirled past as they danced to the music, and the smell of cigar smoke drifted out into the night air. As the evening was mild people sat outside and chatted, but she was careful not to be seen.

All of a sudden her heart missed a beat as she overheard what two people were saying.

'What time do we start filming?' asked a man's voice.

'Early,' answered another man. 'I want to shoot those goats at dawn.'

'It's a trap,' she thought. 'What a rotten low-down trick!' as a scream rose inside her. 'We must get away from here at once,' and she stumbled in a daze towards the stables.

Siobhan was sleeping on her thick mattress of straw, twisting and turning in her sleep for she had indigestion, when Fionuala burst in.

'Quick!' she gasped. 'We must leave this place immediately,' and before Siobhan could say a word she found herself bundled outside and dragged along behind Fionuala who had set off at a shaky run.

It was a beautiful starry night with everything bathed in moonlight and the sound of the river in the air, but the goats were in too much of a hurry to admire its beauty.

At last Fionuala slowed to a walk and told Siobhan what she had heard.

'I don't believe you,' said Siobhan. 'Those people were much too kind to shoot us. Why would they do that anyway?'

'Perhaps they want to make us into stuffed animals
— like that lion,' said Fionuala with a shudder.

There were crossing a large field when they saw
horses quietly grazing in the moonlight. They were
very beautiful, with long flowing manes and tails, and
as the two goats approached they raised their heads
and looked at them.

'Where have you come from?' asked a fine, grey
horse.

'We have had a narrow escape,' said Fionuala, and
she told them what had happened. When she had
finished, the horses roared with laughter.

'You are a pair of silly goats,' they said. 'You weren't
going to be shot; you were going to be filmed. That's
how they talk around here. We have been shot many
times.'

'Are you famous?' asked Siobhan.

'Indeed we are,' answered the grey horse. 'They
made a film about us once called *Butterfly Summer*.
Did you see it?'

'No we didn't,' answered Fionuala. 'We don't care
much for that kind of thing.'

'I do,' said Siobhan. 'I like films very much and
if you hadn't run off like that in such a stupid way,
I'd have been in one. I could have been a star,' and
she burst into tears.

'Well go back then,' said Fionuala. 'Off you go. No
one is stopping you.'

At that moment a strange yowling came from a
corner of the field, followed by the sound of a drum
being beaten loudly.

'What's that?' said Fionuala.

'Is it Indians?' asked Siobhan nervously.

'It's those dratted cats,' answered the grey horse. 'We never get a minute's peace with their noise.'

'What are they doing?' asked Fionuala.

'You may well ask,' said the grey horse. 'They think they are a pop group and sometimes they keep that racket up all night. They were in a film once. They did a bit of singing and drumming, and they've been doing it ever since. They call themselves the Tom-Toms. More like the Caterwaulers if you ask me.'

'Are there any other animals around here who have been in films?' asked Siobhan.

'Indeed there are,' said the horse. 'Too many of them, all thinking they are stars, but the only real stars are us horses.'

Siobhan looked at the beautiful film star horses and she longed to be like them, but as she watched Fionuala disappearing into the darkness she ran after her calling, 'Wait for me! Wait for me!'

The goats followed the river bank, and not another word did they say until they saw the otter. He was standing at the edge of the river, and as they drew near he dived deep into the swift flowing water. After a few minutes he came up again, and in his mouth he held a shining silver fish.

'That's a clever fellow,' said Fionuala in admiration, and up she went to speak to him. But the otter was enjoying his supper, so he told her in no uncertain way to move on.

'No manners,' said Fionuala in disgust.

On the goats journeyed, through big fields and small, through dark spooky woods where the trees cast long shadows and owls called, and Siobhan squeaked and squealed in fright, and all the time the river sang and tumbled near by.

As morning approached, dark clouds rolled up and the rain came pouring down. Now the goats could see the roof tops of Laragh, and where the fields met the road they stopped.

A dark figure stood hunched with his back to the hedge, his long ears drooping in misery. Jacko the donkey was contemplating the dreary morning.

7

Moneystown

'Jacko!' called Fionuala. 'What on earth are *you* doing here,' and she ran up to him in delight.

'So you've come at last,' said Jacko. 'I thought you never would,' and all his misery vanished.

Then he began to talk, and Fionuala began to talk, and when at last they grew silent, neither had heard a word the other had said.

'What stupid creatures they are,' thought Siobhan, as in a sarcastic voice she said, 'Don't let me interrupt you, but I'm going to visit my family now.'

'I'll show you the way,' said Jacko. 'I know just where they live,' and he and Fionuala, still talking, led the way.

'This is most unfortunate,' thought Siobhan, as she followed them. 'The last thing I want is for my aristocratic family to meet these awful old animals.'

Just outside the village of Laragh was a beautiful house, nestling low in gently rolling parkland with many white-fenced paddocks. The rain had stopped, and the early morning sun glinted on its long windows, and the air was filled with the sound of goats' voices, as into the paddocks streamed the Toggenburgs.

'There they are!' cried Siobhan in great excitement. 'My family!' and without as much as a 'good-bye' or a 'thank you' she left Jacko and Fionuala, ran up the avenue and disappeared from sight.

'Well,' said Jacko in disgust, 'she's no lady.' And he and Fionuala passed on and left the house behind.

Then Jacko told Fionuala all that had happened to him since they parted, and it wasn't a lot, and Fionuala told Jacko all that had happened to her, and it was a great deal.

'Now,' said Jacko, 'we will go to Wicklow and join the circus, for that is why I have searched the whole countryside for you.'

'And what would I do in a circus?' said Fionuala with a laugh. 'Have you forgotten that I'm going to Glendalough to find my family?'

'You can find your family later,' said Jacko, 'but the circus is not to be missed. We'll do a double act. You will dance and I'll sing.'

'The last time I danced,' said Fionuala, 'I fell down on the road and got all knocked out.'

'You just need practice,' said Jacko. 'You could be a very good dancer, and I'm sure the circus would give us a job.'

As they talked Fionuala and Jacko crossed a wooden bridge which rattled and banged under their feet, and they took the road that climbed steeply between tall trees which blotted out the sunshine.

'Do you know the way to Wicklow?' she asked.

'Of course I do,' he answered. 'Wasn't I born there?'

As they walked Fionuala thought about the circus, and in her mind she saw written up in coloured lights, 'FIONUALA THE DANCING GOAT', and excitement ran through her and she started to dance.

'Very good!' said Jacko. 'Very good indeed!' as she twirled and whirled along the road. Indeed, she got so carried away that she tripped over a stone, and after that she was more careful with her steps.

'What are you going to sing?' she asked Jacko when she stopped to draw breath.

'I need some new songs,' said Jacko. 'Do you know any?'

'I know one about a goat,' said Fionuala and she started to sing in a very flat voice:

> *Once there was a goat,*
> *A very pretty goat,*
> *Tra-la-la-la-la-la, tra-la-la-la,*
> *Tra-la-la-la.*
>
> *Once there was a goat,*
> *A very clever goat,*
> *Tra-la-la-la-la-la, tra-la-la-la,*
> *Tra-la-la-la*
>
> *Once there was a goat,*
> *A very . . .*

'Pardon me,' said Jacko loudly, 'but I'm getting a little tired of that song. Do you know one about a donkey?'

'Indeed I do,' said Fionuala, and she began to sing again:

> *Once there was a donkey,*
> *And he was very wonky,*
> *Tra-la . . .*

'Stop!' said Jacko. 'You needn't be insulting.'

'I didn't mean to insult you,' said Fionuala. 'That song just came into my head.'

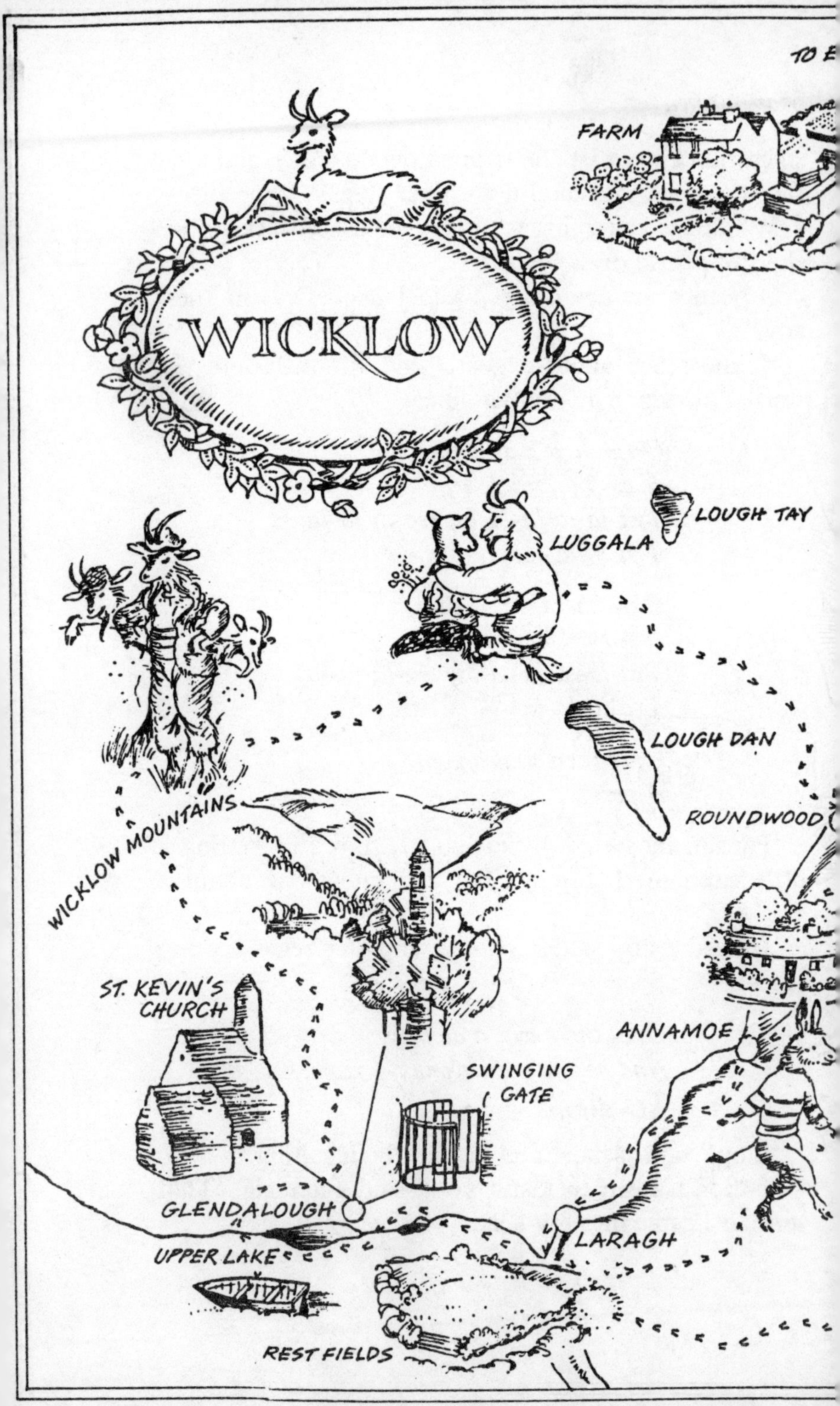

WICKLOW

TO E

FARM

LUGGALA

LOUGH TAY

LOUGH DAN

ROUNDWOOD

WICKLOW MOUNTAINS

ST. KEVIN'S CHURCH

ANNAMOE

SWINGING GATE

GLENDALOUGH

LARAGH

UPPER LAKE

REST FIELDS

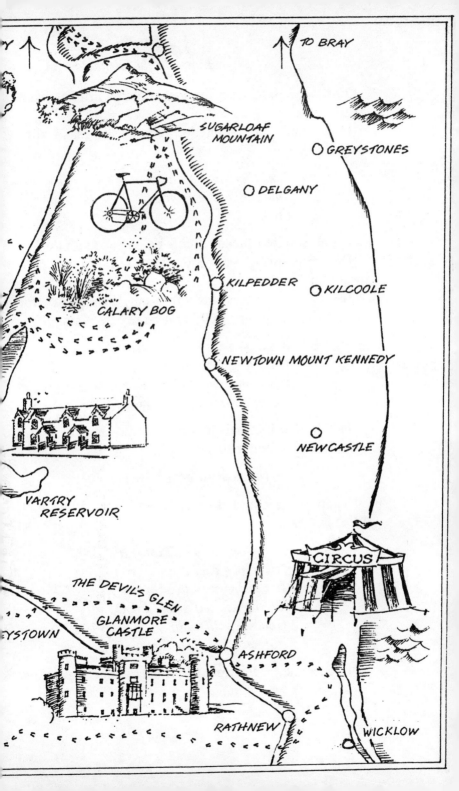

On they walked, with Fionuala doing a little jig from time to time.

'How would this song do, Jacko?' she asked after a while.

> *Once there was an ass,*
> *And he was eating grass,*
> *Tra-la . . .*

'STOP!' shouted Jacko. 'I *hate* being called an ass.'

'I'm very sorry,' said Fionuala. 'I didn't mean to upset you.'

'I think I had better sing *Tipperary*,' said Jacko, 'for I know that song very well,' and he began to sing:

> *It's a long way to Tipperary,*
> *It's a long way to go,*
> *It's a long way to Tipperary,*
> *To the sweetest girl I know . . .*

'Jacko,' said Fionuala before he could sing any more, 'wouldn't it be better to sing:

> *To the sweetest* goat *I know*

'I suppose I could do that,' said Jacko doubtfully. 'I'll start again.'

> *It's a long way to Tipperary,*
> *It's a long way to go,*
> *It's a long way to Tipperary,*
> *To the sweetest goat I know,*
> *Good-bye Piccadilly,*
> *Farewell Leicester Square . . .*

'Excuse me,' interrupted Fionuala. 'Where are those

places? I've never heard of Piccadilly or Leicester
Square.'

'In England,' said Jacko. 'London, I think.'

'Why do you want to sing about England?' said
Fionuala. 'You should sing about *Ireland*. What about
this?'

> *Good-bye Kilmacanogue,*
> *Farewell Annamoe . . .*

'That's good,' said Jacko. 'I like that. I'll start all
over again.'

> *It's a long way to Tipperary,*
> *It's a long way to go,*
> *It's a long way to Tipperary,*
> *To the sweetest goat I know.*
> *Good-bye Kilmacanogue*
> *Farewell Annamoe.*
> *It's a long long way to Tipperary,*
> *But that's where I'll go.*

And Jacko sang his new song over and over again,
and Fionuala danced a very pretty dance over and over
again, and the miles slipped away.

They passed the Vale of Clara, and stopped to look
down on the tumbling river which rushed under the
old stone bridge, and at the little church which stood
almost at the water's edge. The road climbed steeply
between dark silent woods, until they came to a cross-
roads where they turned left for Moneystown.

'Is everyone rich at Moneystown?' asked Fionuala
as they drew near the village.

'Very rich I imagine,' said Jacko. 'It's probably the

richest village in Ireland.'

And Fionuala's thoughts immediately turned to houses with swimming-pools and posh cars.

They passed Punt's Pub and Penny's Supermarket, which had a sign in the window saying, 'Free Draw Tonight', and they came to Coyne's garage. Lying around outside were piles of scrap metal and old tyres and a rusty petrol pump with a notice stuck on it, 'Get your free tea-towels here'.

And then Fionuala saw the car. It was the most beautiful car she had ever seen, black and shiny and almost as big as a house. It was in a field right beside the garage, and sitting on top of it was a large brown hen.

'Look Jacko,' she said. 'Did you ever see the likes of that?' And being an inquisitive goat she just had to find out why the hen was sitting on top of such a car.

'I live here,' said the hen, 'and so do they.' She pointed inside to where a crowd of hens sat crooning softly to themselves.

'You live in great luxury,' said Fionuala in awe.

'You should see where Mrs Price's ducks live,' answered the hen. 'They have a whole caravan all to themselves, and Mr Richie's dogs have chairs and a mattress in the garden. Even the sheep have bed-ends for gates, and the cows drink water from a real bath. People have money to throw away nowadays, and when they get tired of something they just chuck it out. You could fill a house with the things people get rid of, just left lying around for anyone to take.'

Fionuala and Jacko walked on until they came to the Post Office. A van was drawn up outside and two men were unloading large sacks.

'Is it money?' asked Fionuala.

'Probably,' answered Jacko.

At that moment an old man and a young woman came out of the Post Office.

'Pension day,' said the old man, 'and isn't it grand to get money for doing nothing.'

'It's well for you,' answered the young woman.

'Money grows on trees round here.'

'Did you hear that?' whispered Fionuala. 'This must be a wonderful place to live.'

Further down the road they passed a gate which had 'County Council Pound' written on it and Fionuala peered over it looking for pound notes.

'You won't find any money there,' said Jacko. 'A Pound is where they put poor lost animals,' but Fionuala wasn't listening, for lying right at her feet was a 50p piece.

'I'm surprised everyone in Ireland doesn't live here,' she said as she picked it up.

'You should leave that money where you found it,' said Jacko. 'It doesn't belong to you.'

'It does now,' said Fionuala. 'Everything's free in Moneystown. All you have to do is find something and it's yours.'

Fionuala was so busy talking that she nearly fell over a little basket lying on the grass verge. It was the nicest basket she had even seen with a little lid which opened and closed, and inside on a bed of straw were three shiny one-pound coins.

'Look at this!' she cried. 'We've been given a basket to carry our money,' and she put the 50p in with the pound coins.

'You can't take that,' said Jacko, greatly upset. 'Put it back, Fionuala. Nobody leaves baskets full of money lying around for anyone to take.'

'Oh yes they do, in Moneystown,' called Fionuala as down the road she skipped.

'Free Range Eggs' said a sign at the farmyard.

'We'll get some of those free eggs, Jacko,' said

Fionuala. 'They would fit beautifully in this little basket.'

Just then a white van shot round the corner and drew up in front of the farmyard. It came so fast that Fionuala and Jacko leaped into the ditch in fright.

The driver blew his horn loudly and out of the front door came the farmer's wife carrying a tray of new-laid eggs.

'I'm in a great hurry today,' said the man as he put the eggs carefully into the van. 'The supermarket in Rathdrum wants extra eggs and they want them fast.'

'Here's someone else who wants you fast,' said the farmer's wife, as a young boy came running up the road waving and calling.

'My mam says you didn't leave her the egg money,' he panted. 'And you've taken her basket too.'

'I did no such thing,' answered the van man angrily. 'I put three one-pound coins inside the basket and left it where I always do, at the side of the road.'

'Well then it's been stolen,' said the boy. 'My mam is in a real temper about it.'

'Don't blame me,' said the van man, and he drove off at top speed.

'I'd go to the guards if I were you,' said the farmer's wife. 'There must be some old tramp around. Probably down from Dublin.' She hurried into the house, and the boy slowly made his way back up the road.

'Now!' said Jacko. 'See what you've done taking that basket. A right mess we're in. We'll have the guards after us and end up in prison yet.'

'What are we to do?' wailed Fionuala.

'What *you* are going to do,' said Jacko, 'is to put

the basket back where you found it, and *I'm* going
to stay right here.'

'Oh Jacko,' said Fionuala, greatly alarmed. 'I
couldn't do that all on my own. You'll *have* to come
with me.'

Which of course, being a nice fellow, is what he
did!

'The trouble with you, Fionuala,' he said as they
left the village of Moneystown, 'is that you always think
you are right.'

'Well I wasn't right about that place,' said Fionuala
airily. 'Moneystown is a poor sort of village. Not a
rich town at all!'

8

The Devil's Glen

After Fionuala and Jacko left Moneystown they
trudged along wearily, for their adventure had made
them tired.

'I'm starving,' said Fionuala at last. 'If we don't eat
soon I will faint from hunger.' So they stopped to graze
along the grass verge. Now and then a car passed, and
Fionuala jumped with fright in case it was the guards
searching for her.

'Is it far to Wicklow?' she asked Jacko time and
again, at every corner they turned.

'Quite far,' answered Jacko. Never had the miles
passed so slowly or the day seemed so long, but at
last the shadows lengthened and evening drew near.

'We won't get to Wicklow tonight,' said Jacko. 'We
must stop soon and find a place to rest.'

Past Tiglin, they stumbled down the steep hill until
they came to Glanmore stables. In through the gate
and under the archway turned Jacko, with Fionuala
following, but when they got inside they found the
whole place was in ruins, with only the outside walls
standing. Brambles and weeds grew wild in the cobbled
yard, and the beautiful oval windows, where the glass
had long ago broken and fallen, gaped like black holes
in the gathering dusk.

'We can't stay here,' gasped Fionuala in horror, as
a bat swooped past and darkness fell.

'I can't go a step further,' answered Jacko, 'for I'm dead beat,' and indeed the poor old donkey looked about to drop.

They stood with their backs to the crumbling walls while the wind whined round them, dark clouds scudded across the moon and ghostly shadows lurked in the darkness.

'Who owned this place?' asked Fionuala nervously, as she moved closer to Jacko.

'Long ago,' said Jacko, 'these stables were full of horses, and they all belonged to the Synges who lived at Glanmore Castle, just half a mile from here. One of that family was the famous playwright, John Millington Synge, and when he was a boy he spent his holidays at Glanmore Castle.'

'How do you know all this?' asked Fionuala, much impressed by Jacko's knowledge.

'I know it because my grandfather lived here once,' said Jacko. 'He pulled a beautiful trap, and when the weather was fine he took the children all over the countryside, up to Annamoe and Roundwood, and even down to Wicklow.

'All went well until one day he refused to take them home. He just stopped in the middle of the road, and nothing would make him budge.'

'Why did he do that?' asked Fionuala in surprise.

'I suppose he was fed up pulling the trap. I believe the children had to walk home, and when a groom went to collect my grandfather, he bit him so hard he couldn't sit down for a week!'

'What happened to your grandfather then?' asked Fionuala.

'They sold him to a farmer down in Wicklow,' answered Jacko. 'There was no more living in grand stables for him. It was all work from then on, and many's the time he regretted his hasty action in biting that groom.'

'What was your grandfather called?' asked Fionuala.

'Singsong,' answered Jacko. 'I believe he had a very fine voice.'

As they talked the rain began to fall and soon the two animals were very wet indeed. Jacko didn't seem to mind, and after a while he fell fast asleep, but Fionuala stood huddled, wide-awake, wet and miserable. There were strange sounds in the place, unexplained rustlings and squeakings, and once she was sure she heard horses' hooves on the cobbles, but as she listened with fast-beating heart the only sound was the wind as it moaned through the broken walls.

After a time the rain stopped and the moon appeared, and something large and white glided past in the cold light. She cried out in alarm but it was only an owl, which disappeared into the darkness with a screech.

All night long she shivered and shook with cold and fear, but the night passed and as a faint light appeared in the sky, she at last slept.

When she awoke, Jacko was busy eating the brambles and nettles which grew everywhere, and nearby a little wren sang at the top of her voice.

'Good-morning,' said Jacko. 'I hope you slept well.'

'I hardly slept at all,' answered Fionuala crossly. 'I was wet and cold all night. I don't know why we had to stay in this awful old ruin.'

'I think it is a very nice place,' said Jacko. 'I can just imagine my grandfather going in and out of these stables, and how splendid they must have been. I would very much like to live here.'

'Well I wouldn't,' snapped Fionuala. 'I've never spent a more uncomfortable night in my whole life.'

'Well,' said Jacko, 'I've had many homes, some good and some bad, but one thing I have never had is a nice warm stable.'

Then Fionuala was sorry she had spoken crossly and she felt sadness for the hard life Jacko had led.

The bell of Nun's Cross Church was ringing as Fionuala and Jacko came to the Devil's Glen.

'I wouldn't like to live in this place,' said Fionuala,

'with the devil roaming around.'

'The devil isn't here at all,' said Jacko. 'But my cousins are and I want to pay them a visit.'

'Do you think it's safe?' asked Fionuala as they left the road and began to walk through the dark woods of the Devil's Glen.

'You do ask some funny questions,' said Jacko. 'I've never met such a nervous goat. You'd even be afraid of your own shadow.'

'I'm afraid of nothing,' said Fionuala. And to show how brave she was she walked quickly ahead. But when a pheasant flew up with a loud squawk, she fell back with a scream.

Now the trees were close together, almost blotting out the sky. Tiny green siskins flitted twittering high amongst the branches, while down below in the damp earth strange shaped toadstools and dark mosses grew everywhere.

A mink ran across the path and turned his bad-tempered face towards Fionuala and Jacko as he looked at them before running on into the undergrowth, and a herd of deer appeared and disappeared silently through the trees.

They came to a lake where ducks swam and flew quacking overhead in the still morning air. Two swans glided by, dipping their long necks into the water as they searched for food, while at the lake edge a little moorhen walked in the mud, and the air was full of bird song.

'Where do your cousins live?' asked Fionuala as she and Jacko left the lake and walked again through the woods.

'Somewhere around here,' answered Jacko. 'I'm sure we will find them soon.'

They came to a wide path which twisted and turned, and in the distance they saw a house. It stood all by itself in a clearing in the wood, surrounded by a beautiful garden with lawns and flowers and a little stream. The air was filled with the sound of bees as they flew from flower to flower, whose perfume drifted on the warm air.

Lying outside the open front door in the sunshine were six cats, and playing on the green lawn were six dogs. A pair of rabbits sat outside their hutch eating lettuce leaves and Fionuala thought that in all her life she had never seen such a happy place.

'Do your cousins live here?' she asked hopefully.

'I don't think so,' answered Jacko, 'but I'm sure they are close by,' and Fionuala and Jacko passed that beautiful place and entered the woods again. Now the air felt chill and damp, and they could hear rushing water as they came to the river. It tossed and tumbled over rocks and stones as it carried whole tree branches along.

Fionuala would have turned back but Jacko walked briskly on, and with a fearful look at those dark waters she hurried after him.

The air was filled with the noise of the angry river, and then they heard another noise, a great roaring which grew louder with every step. There right in front of them, gushing and cascading over the high cliff wall, came a waterfall. Fionuala had never seen anything like it before; even Jacko stood in awe watching the sheet of falling water.

They were still watching the waterfall when they heard another sound. It started on a low note and went higher and higher, until the whole air was filled with it, a great howling which echoed round and round the woods and then died away, only to start all over again.

'It's the devil,' cried Fionuala, and she fainted clean away.

When she came to, Jacko was looking down at her in great anxiety, and standing beside him was the biggest dog Fionuala had ever seen. He had a rough grey coat and he was almost as tall as Jacko.

She looked at the huge dog, and the dog looked at her. Then bending down he gently licked her face as he said, 'I'm sorry to have frightened you with my howling, but I thought I was going to die of loneliness.'

Fionuala managed to stand up and she had a drink

of cold river water. Then, when she felt quite better, the big dog told her and Jacko his story.

'I was born in Dublin,' said the dog, 'and when I was six weeks old I went to a very nice home. I had three little children to play with and a nice bed to sleep in, and everyone made a great fuss of me.

'And then a terrible thing happened. I grew too big. I grew and I grew and, no matter what I did, I just got bigger and bigger.

'Then the three little children said I was too big to play with, and their mother said I was too big for the house and their father said I was too big for the garden.

'So one day he put me in the car, and told the children he was taking me for a nice drive. I was so excited I could hardly sit still. We drove a long way and then we walked and walked, and we didn't stop until we came to this very waterfall.

'Then the father gave me a lovely bone to eat, but when I had finished eating it he had quite disappeared. I searched and searched for him all day, and I ran and ran through the woods, but he never came back and I can't think what happened to him.'

'This dog has been dumped,' whispered Jacko to Fionuala. 'I know about that kind of thing. It happens to dogs all the time.'

'What do you mean "dumped"?' asked Fionuala in a low voice.

'That man brought him here and lost him on purpose,' said Jacko. 'And all because he grew too big.'

'Are you sure?' asked Fionuala in horror. 'His family sound nice enough.'

'Nice or not,' answered Jacko, 'that is what some people do.'

'I want to go home,' said the big dog. 'I want to play with those little children, and I want my own bed, and I'm terribly hungry,' and he began to sob loudly.

'What are we to do?' said Fionuala, greatly distressed. 'We can't leave this poor dog here. We will have to take him with us. Perhaps he could join the circus too.'

After a while and much comforting, the dog's sobs grew less and finally stopped.

'Can you do any acts,' asked Fionuala, 'like singing or dancing?'

'I can chase a ball,' said the dog. 'I'm very good at that for I had a lovely ball at my home.'

'Have you got a name?' asked Jacko.

'I have,' answered the dog, 'but you might laugh if I tell you what it is.'

'We won't laugh,' said Fionuala.

'It's Goofy,' answered the poor dog, and he hung his head in shame.

'We'll give you a new name,' said Fionuala. 'What would you like to be called?'

'I don't know,' said the dog. 'But I would love a new name.'

'We'll call you Brian, after Brian Boru, High King of Ireland,' said Fionuala.

How pleased Brian was with his new name as he said it over and over again.

Suddenly Jacko had an idea.

'We will take Brian to that beautiful house we

passed,' he said. 'For whoever lives there must be very
fond of animals.'

So they left the thundering waterfall behind, and
they left the dark rushing river, and they walked
through the tall trees until they came to the clearing
in the woods, and there was the house, just as before,
with the six cats lying in the sunshine, and the six
dogs playing on the lawn, and the two rabbits still
eating crisp lettuce leaves, the air still filled with the
sound of bees.

As Fionuala, Jacko and Brian stood watching that
happy place, a lady came out of the open front door
and looked at them.

'Hello,' she said, 'I'm Margaret. Who are you?'

Then Jacko told her Brian's story.

'Of course he may stay here,' she said. 'He is a
beautiful Irish wolfhound and I will be glad to give
him a home.'

'I didn't know I was an Irish wolfhound,' said Brian,
'I thought I was just a too-big dog.'

'You are nothing of the kind,' answered Margaret.
'You are a noble animal and in ancient times you were
the dog of the Kings of Ireland.'

'You see, I was right,' whispered Fionuala.

How happy Brian was then! He rolled over and over
in delight on the beautiful green grass, and the six dogs
ran up to meet him and soon they were all playing
together. Brian chased round and round and he wasn't
one bit too big for that garden.

As the dogs played Margaret talked to Fionuala and
Jacko, and she told them many sad stories.

'Do you see that little black dog?' she said, pointing

to a tiny dog who pounced and jumped as she played with Brian. 'She was thrown out of a car by people who didn't want her. And that brown and white dog with the long woolly coat was left like Brian, here in the woods.'

'How can people do such cruel things?' asked Fionuala, very upset.

'That I cannot tell you,' answered Margaret. 'For all they have to do is contact the Prevention of Cruelty to Animals who will find new homes for any unwanted animals.'

'What will you do if Brian's owner comes back?' asked Jacko.

'He won't come back,' said Margaret. 'But if he does I will report him for cruelty.'

The day wore on and Jacko and Fionuala got ready to leave.

'Stay until tomorrow,' said Margaret, 'for tonight we will have a party.' And what a party it was! There was a bonfire on the lawn, and presents, and a treasure hunt, and all kinds of food for all kinds of animals, for the squirrels and the rabbits came from the woods, and the hedgehogs and the field-mice and even the deer crept shyly into the garden. The fun and games lasted until the stars grew pale and dawn drew near.

Then Margaret made a cosy bed for Fionuala and Jacko in a warm shed, for the dawn air was cold, and Brian had a beautiful kennel all for himself, and everyone fell asleep and didn't waken until the sun was high.

'We must leave now,' said Jacko as they said good-bye to Brian who was playing with a lovely new ball.

'Good-bye and thank you,' said Brian. 'I am very happy in my new home, but my old home was nice too.'

'That's the thing about dogs,' said Jacko as he and Fionuala left the Devil's Glen. 'They'll never say a bad word about anyone.'

They took the road to Ashford in the morning sunshine, and then turned to pass Hunter's Hotel. They paused at the garden gate where people sat at little green tables drinking coffee, and Fionuala would have lingered but Jacko urged her on. Through the village of Rathnew and along the busy main road they trotted, as people stared and pointed from passing cars.

As they drew near Wicklow, a sudden thought struck Fionuala.

'Jacko,' she said, 'you never found your cousins.'

'They've moved,' said Jacko. 'Margaret told me, Jackeen has gone to Arklow and Kojack to Bray.'

On Fionuala and Jacko journeyed until at last they came to Wicklow.

9

Wicklow

'Fáilte' said the sign at the entrance to the town.

'What does *Fáilte* mean?' asked Fionuala.

'And you who knows all about Ireland. Don't you know any *Irish*?' said Jacko in amazement. 'It means "Welcome".'

'Of course I know what it means,' said Fionuala with a toss of her head. 'I just wondered if *you* knew.'

Jacko took the road to the Murrough and the sea.

'Will we not go into the town?' asked Fionuala in disappointment, for she had hoped to look at the shops.

'Certainly not,' said Jacko. 'I've no intention of getting caught up in traffic jams and the like. This is the way to go.'

They passed a school where boys and girls were throwing a big ball to one another and Fionuala stopped to watch. It was nice brown ball and she would have loved to join in, but she remembered what had happened at the tennis party in Annamoe when she played with the little white ball, and with a shudder she walked on quickly.

They passed the station and came to the Metal Bridge over the River Vartry. Fionuala leaned over the bridge to see the water rushing and swirling underneath. A redshank flew screaming by and two swans, with feathers fluffed out to catch the breeze, sailed under the archways and on up the lakes. As Fionuala turned to watch them, she saw Sugarloaf Mountain in the distance, and for a moment she felt homesick.

'Come on,' called Jacko. 'Be quick, for there is a train coming.'

Fionuala had been so busy watching the river that she hadn't heard the rumble of the train as it drew nearer and nearer. Now as she looked up she saw it approaching on the track beside the bridge where she was standing, and she nearly died of fright, for she had never seen a train before.

'Help me,' she screamed. 'Jacko! Save me!' and she threw herself down on her knees and covered her head with her front feet, as the train thundered by, hooting and clanking, into Wicklow station.

When at last Fionuala dared to look up, all was silent but of Jacko there was no sign.

'Jacko,' she called, 'where are you?' But her voice came out only in a hoarse whisper. At last she managed to stand up and stagger across the bridge. As she reached the far end she saw Jacko. At least she saw the tip of one of his long ears, for he was standing underneath the bridge with his feet in the water.

'What are you doing down there?' she called. 'And why didn't you wait for me? That creature nearly got me.'

'What creature?' asked Jacko, coming out from under the bridge. 'What are you talking about?'

'The Dragon, of course,' said Fionuala. 'If I hadn't knelt down so that he couldn't see me, he would have eaten me alive. He roared and screamed as he went by and his hot breath blew all over me. I never saw anything like it in my whole life.'

'That was no dragon,' said Jacko. 'That was a train, a very ordinary train.'

'I don't believe you,' said Fionuala. 'It was a dragon and that's why you ran away and left me. I must say I don't think you are much of a friend.'

'I didn't run away and leave you,' said Jacko. 'I just don't like the noise of trains; it hurts my ears.'

Fionuala stood and looked at Jacko and many thoughts went through her head, but at last she had to ask the question. 'What is a train?' she said.

'A train carries people,' answered Jacko.

'Well I'm glad I'm not people,' said Fionuala and off she went at a fast walk towards the Murrough.

Now they could see the big blue and white circus tent with flags flying gently in the breeze and Fionuala began to feel very excited.

Then she saw the Sea. The circus was on a broad green stretch of grass at the water's edge and beyond was the harbour, with Wicklow town rising up the hill behind. It was very beautiful, but Fionuala was filled with dread. She remembered how she and Siobhan had stood on top of Sugarloaf Mountain and seen the Sea, and how they had wondered if it was the Edge of the World.

'I don't think I can go any further,' she said in a small voice.

'Now what's wrong with you?' asked Jacko. 'What are you afraid of this time?'

'The Sea,' whispered Fionuala. 'I think we must be at the Edge of the World.'

'What nonsense you talk,' said Jacko in astonishment. 'Of course it's not the edge of the world. Over there,' pointing, 'is Wales, and beyond that England, and then more sea and more countries, and on and on, it never ends. Don't you know anything about the world? You must have lived a very quiet life on Sugarloaf Farm.'

'We led a very exciting life there,' said Fionuala indignantly. 'We went to shows and all kinds of events.'

'I went to a show once myself,' said Jacko. 'But I didn't think much of it, to tell the truth.'

'I expect you didn't win any prizes,' said Fionuala.

'You're right there,' said Jacko. 'But it didn't worry me one bit. A lot of fuss about nothing, if you ask me.'

'I quite agree,' said Fionuala. 'Stuck-up lot of creatures at shows, and as for judges, they are quite disgusting characters.'

As they talked Fionuala and Jacko walked along the green stretch of grass called the Murrough, towards the circus. As they drew near they could see caravans and cages for the animals, and in the middle of it all was the big tent.

'It looks wonderful,' said Fionuala, quickening her pace. 'Hurry up, Jacko!'

But Jacko wouldn't hurry. In fact he had stopped

walking altogether, for now that they had finally arrived he was feeling nervous.

'I think we'll stop here for a while,' he said to Fionuala. 'I feel like a swim.'

'You're not going in there?' Fionuala anxiously looked at the water where waves splashed on the stony shore.

'Perhaps just a paddle,' said Jacko. 'It might be a little rough to swim today,' and down to the water's edge he meandered.

Fionuala watched in horror as he walked up and down, knee-deep in the sea, and she closed her eyes tight when once or twice waves splashed right over him. When at last he left the water and returned to sit on the shore beside her, his black coat was quite wet.

'I think you are very brave, Jacko,' she said, in admiration.

'Not a bit of it,' he answered. 'The sea is in my blood, for my ancestors were more at home on the water than out of it.'

'What do you mean?' she asked in alarm. 'How can the sea be in your blood?'

'Well it's like this.' He lowered his voice and looked right and left, and behind him, to make sure no one was listening. 'My great-great-great-grandfather, many times removed, was a pirate. Jack the Black they called him as he sailed the Seven Seas.'

'A *pirate*!' whispered Fionuala. 'How wonderful to be related to a *pirate*. What did he do? Chop people's heads off and steal their money?'

'He did nothing of the sort,' answered Jacko. 'He

was a nice, kind pirate who sailed round the world doing good. He took from the rich and gave to the poor.'

'What brought him to Ireland? He can't have found many rich people here.'

'Ah,' he said, 'that's a sad story. For he wasn't coming to Ireland at all. His galleon was blown off course by a great storm and he was shipwrecked at this very spot. His crew escaped but he was captured and put in the lowest dungeon at the Black Castle.'

'Where's the Black Castle?' asked Fionuala.

'You're looking at it ... or what's left of it,' and he pointed towards the hill above the harbour where three jagged rocks rose to the sky.

'Many centuries ago the Vikings came to Wicklow and built a great castle at the mouth of the River Vartry. Then the Normans came and the castle was rebuilt. As the years went by fierce battles raged around its walls, and it changed hands many times until at last it was destroyed, and those three rocks are all that is left of it today.'

'What happened to Jack the Black?' asked Fionuala. 'Did he escape or was he left in the Black Castle for ever?'

'Indeed he did escape,' said Jacko. 'It happened like this. The lowest dungeon was really a cave deep down under the castle. All day long the tide came and went, and through the bars of his prison Jack the Black watched it.

'One night the tide rose higher and higher, and the wind blew stronger and stronger, and the waves came flooding into the cave. He thought he'd drown as he clung to the bars of his prison gate.

'Then came a wave bigger and stronger than all the rest. It roared into the cave and slammed against the prison bars and, lo and behold, what with the weight of Jack the Black clinging to it and the hinges being old and rusty, the gate was washed clean away.

'Jack the Black was a strong swimmer, so all he had to do was swim out of the cave and into the sea beyond. The night was dark and without a moon, and as he was tossed this way and that in the mighty waves, he didn't know in which direction to swim for the shore.

'Suddenly the clouds parted, the moon shone down, and there right beside him was a flight of steps. Using all his strength he pulled himself out of the water. The steps were wet and slippy, and very difficult for a donkey to climb, but climb them he did, and so he escaped.

'I believe he had many adventures before he was safe, but at last he reached the Wicklow Hills where he found sanctuary. He also found the rest of his crew. And that is how the first Spanish donkeys came to Ireland.'

'What happened to his boat?' asked Fionuala.

'Sunk!' said Jacko. 'With a hold full of gold and silver, and it all lies just out there,' and he pointed to the entrance to Wicklow harbour. 'Many people have tried to find it but no one has ever succeeded.'

'You must be very proud of your ancestor,' said Fionuala.

'Indeed I am,' answered Jacko. 'And I believe I look exactly like him.'

10

The Circus

Fionuala and Jacko had talked so long that the sun was setting when they made their way along the Murrough towards the circus. As they drew near they heard music and laughter, for the evening performance had begun. There was noise and bustle everywhere and from the caravans' windows lights shone out. They stood in the shadows and watched.

A man went by leading two camels who wore richly embroidered saddle-cloths and coloured halters. Behind them trotted eight white ponies with scarlet plumes on their heads and bridles to match. A little girl, no more than six years old, ran beside them, wearing a gold and silver spangled dress and in her

hand she carried a fairy wand. Next came the clowns with baggy trousers and red noses, pushing and shoving one another, as they made their way into the big tent.

'Oh,' cried Fionuala, 'we *must* go inside and see the circus,' and before Jacko could stop her she ran towards the entrance. At that moment there was a loud bang, and all the lights inside the tent went out as the clowns played a trick on one another. When the lights came on again, they were both inside and no one had even noticed.

They watched as act followed act. There were jugglers who did amazing things with cups and plates, and trapeze artists who flew through the air high above the crowd and brought gasps of wonder from everyone. There was an elephant who could go up and down stairs, and a little black dog who jumped over hurdles.

Six men in gold jackets played happy circus music, and the Ringmaster, wearing a red coat and tall black hat, stood in the middle of the circle cracking his long whip, as the beautiful white ponies trotted and cantered and turned and bowed, and the little girl in the spangled dress rode round and round, and didn't fall off once.

Hundreds of coloured lights blazed down and Fionuala had never seen anything so wonderful. There was even a lion who played a drum and a tiger who kicked a football, but best of all she liked the clowns.

'What do you get if you cross a kangaroo with a sheep?' asked Jingo.

'A woolly jumper,' shouted Bingo.

'And what happens to a sheep-dog who drinks too much?'

'He gets the collie-wobbles,' roared Bingo.

The crowd laughed and clapped as the two clowns rolled and tumbled and chased one another, here, there and everywhere. Fionuala laughed louder than anyone and the tears ran down her cheeks.

'Now, boys and girls,' said Jingo. 'Here's a riddle for you— and the first one who answers correctly can come into the ring and help with our next trick. Listen carefully: "What did Dracula say to his girl friend?"'

But although the boys and girls shouted many answers, no one was correct.

Suddenly Jingo looked straight at Fionuala and he called out, 'I think I hear a correct answer from that lady in the black and white coat. Dracula said to his girl friend, "I'm batty about you." Thank you, Madam, would you kindly step this way.'

'Quick!' said Jacko. 'Let's get out of here!' and before Fionuala knew what was happening, he had pulled her out of the tent.

'Why did you do that?' she asked. 'I would love to have helped the clowns with their next trick.'

'Are you daft?' said Jacko. 'The moment they saw you were a goat we would have been in big trouble, and that would have been the end of our double act. Anyway you didn't answer the riddle. You didn't say a word.'

'I was just going to,' said Fionuala, 'because I'm very good at riddles.'

From inside the tent came a loud roll of drums as the circus ended. Out through the entrance poured the audience on their way home.

'We will wait until all these people have gone,' said Jacko. 'Then we will look for the owner of the circus.'

It was a beautiful night and Fionuala and Jacko stood looking out over the calm sea. The moon had risen and was casting a broad track on the water. At the harbour a lighthouse winked on and off, while the lights of the town twinkled and shone in the darkness.

Fionuala felt very peaceful and quite tired after all the excitement of the circus and she yawned once or twice.

It took a long time for the audience to go home. They hung around the caravans, and looked into the cages where the animals were being bedded down for the night. At last everywhere grew silent, but when Jacko and Fionuala looked for the circus folk, they too had all disappeared.

'Now what are we to do?' said Fionuala. 'There is no one left to audition us?'

At that moment a man went by carrying two buckets

which clanked and banged as he walked.

'Excuse me,' called Jacko, 'but could you please tell us where we can find the owner of the circus?'

The man stopped and looked at Fionuala and Jacko in surprise.

'What are you two doing here?' he asked.

'We are looking for a job in the circus,' said Jacko. 'My friend and I would like to be auditioned.'

'You will have to see Mr Hurry Harry,' answered the man. 'But you won't get him tonight for he'd be fast asleep by now. Come back in the morning. I'd be off home if I were you.'

'We can't do that,' said Jacko, 'for we have travelled many miles to get here.'

The man looked carefully at Fionuala and Jacko, and what he saw was a poor old goat and a worn-out donkey, and because he was a kind fellow he took pity on them.

'Look,' he said, 'it just so happens that there is an empty trailer tonight. It's not very comfortable but if you like you can sleep there.'

The trailer was indeed uncomfortable and not very clean, but the kind man put some straw on the floor and gave Fionuala and Jacko a bit of hay to eat and a bucket of water to drink. The hay was a little musty and the water a little stale, but they were so hungry and thirsty they ate every scrap and drank every drop, and then Jacko fell fast asleep and began to snore.

But Fionuala couldn't sleep. Her mind was full of the sights and sounds of the circus. She thought about Jacko's singing and about her dancing, and she wondered what kind of costume she would be given to wear. Silver and gold like the little girl with the ponies would suit her well, or perhaps blue satin like the trapeze artists.

And then she had a splendid idea. It was such a good idea she just had to waken Jacko to tell him about it. He wasn't at all pleased to be wakened, and he said some quite cross things, but she was so excited about her idea she didn't even hear them.

'Jacko,' she said, 'when we have finished our singing and dancing act, we'll tell jokes. The audience would love that.'

'Do you know any jokes?' asked Jacko crossly.

'No,' said Fionuala, 'but I'm sure I could think of some. In fact I have just thought of one now: What do you get if you cross a goat with a cart?'

'What?' asked Jacko angrily.

'A go-cart,' answered Fionuala, and she roared with laughter.

'That's stupid,' said Jacko. 'We can't tell jokes unless they are good ones.'

'Well,' said Fionuala, 'do *you* know any good ones?'

'I know just one,' answered Jacko. 'Where do donkeys go for their holidays?'

'Where?'

'They go to Bray,' answered Jacko.

'Oh, that's good,' said Fionuala. 'Very good indeed,' and she laughed and laughed.

Suddenly she jumped up. 'I've thought of an even better one than that! If it rained all through the holidays, you could say, "Oh, what an ass I was to come here to bray!" '

As soon as she had said it she remembered that Jacko

hated to be called an ass. Luckily he was distracted by a sudden loud banging on the wall of their trailer until it shivered and shook, for the camels who were asleep next door had been wakened.

'Go to sleep,' said Jacko. 'Because if those fellows get us we won't see the light of day again.'

'Jacko,' whispered Fionuala after a little while. 'I've thought of another joke.'

'We're not going to tell *any* jokes,' said Jacko very angrily. 'Jokes are for clowns, and anyway I don't like all that laughing.'

'Does it hurt your ears?' asked Fionuala.

'It hurts more than my ears,' said Jacko. 'It's something I don't really like talking about, but I'll tell you if you promise never to breathe a word to anyone.

'Long ago, when I was quite young, I was with the Blarney Barney Circus. I became quite famous because I was so good at laughing. Day after day, and night after night, at every performance I laughed, and my name was written up in little coloured lights — JACKO THE LAUGHING JACKASS!'

'What did you laugh at?' asked Fionuala.

'At nothing,' said Jacko. 'Nothing at all.'

'Not at jokes?' asked Fionuala.

'Certainly not at jokes. There were none. I just laughed and laughed until I couldn't laugh any more.'

'How dreadful,' said Fionuala. 'And how very insulting to treat you like that.'

'That's what *I* thought,' answered Jacko sadly. 'So I ran away and joined another circus. And that was when I sang and danced and pulled a little cart full of boys and girls.'

As Jacko finished speaking, a great banging and crashing sounded again on the trailer walls, and the camels next door called out some rude words and gruesome threats. Fionuala and Jacko fell silent with fear and at last they both slept.

It was barely light when the kind man who had given them shelter opened the trailer door and called to them.

'I'd make yourselves scarce,' he said. 'Circus folk are not in the best of tempers early in the morning and Mr Hurry Harry never wakes before 10 o'clock.'

So Fionuala and Jacko walked along the Murrough by the sea and watched the sun rise like a ball of fire over the water. A boat was going fishing and the sound of the engine could be heard in the clear air. Overhead, gulls wheeled and screamed as they fought for scraps of food. A seal popped up his head just off shore and looked at them before diving deep into the dark sea.

As ten o'clock drew near, Fionuala and Jacko made their way back to the circus. The animals were being fed and there was hustle and bustle everywhere.

Mr Hurry Harry's caravan was large and shiny and the door was wide open, letting in the sunshine. A delicious smell of cooking wafted out, and they would have felt very hungry if they hadn't felt so nervous.

Jacko walked bravely up to the open door and knocked.

'Come in,' said a grumpy voice, and in they went.

Inside the caravan sat Mr Hurry Harry. He was having breakfast, and on his knee was the little black dog who could jump over hurdles.

'What do you want?' he asked peevishly when he

saw them. 'Can't you see I'm busy?'

'Please, Sir,' said Jacko. 'We would like to be auditioned. My friend and I do a very good double act.'

'What do you do?' snapped Mr Hurry Harry.

'We sing and dance,' answered Jacko.

'Well, get on with it then,' said Mr Hurry Harry. 'I haven't all day to waste,' and he stuffed a large piece of toast into his mouth.

So Jacko started to sing *Tipperary*, but he was so nervous he got everything muddled. He sang all the wrong words and he forgot the bit about the sweetest goat.

Fionuala danced and danced, but there wasn't much room in the caravan for twists and twirls, and when she tried a few high kicks she knocked the cup and saucer out of Mr Hurry Harry's hand. The little black

dog started to bark, and he even tried to bite Fionuala as she whirled around and around.

'That's enough,' shouted Mr Hurry Harry when the noise of singing, dancing and barking grew deafening. 'I don't need to see any more.'

'Well, what do you think?' gasped Fionuala as she tried to get her breath back. 'Have you got a job for us in the circus?'

'Oh yes,' replied Mr Hurry Harry. 'I have a job for you all right. Wait here while I get Slow Joe. He'll look after you,' and out of the caravan he shuffled.

A few minutes later a little man with a face like a monkey jumped into the caravan.

'Come with me,' he said. 'I'll get you all fixed up for work.' Fionuala and Jacko couldn't believe their luck as they followed Slow Joe, who raced along so fast they had to run to keep up with him.

Fionuala caught sight of some beautiful costumes hanging up in the caravans as they sped along, but Slow Joe didn't stop until he came to a little shed behind the circus tent. She couldn't believe her eyes when he handed her a dirty apron and a scrubbing brush, and Jacko a grimy overall, a bucket and a shovel.

'Wh-a-t are th-e-se for?' she stuttered in alarm.

'For work of course,' answered Slow Joe. 'Look sharp now and get on with it, for you and the old ass are to clean the animals' cages. Mind you do it properly, for Mr. Hurry Harry doesn't like slipshod work.'

And that is just what Fionuala and Jacko did, all day long. They scrubbed and brushed and cleaned until they were quite exhausted. It was dangerous work too, for they had to be quick with the cleaning when the animals were in the tent rehearsing. Fionuala had a narrow escape when the camels returned as she was scrubbing their cage. They were still angry with her and Jacko for making them lose their sleep. She had to get out of their cage in a hurry, because they made some nasty threatening gestures.

But she had a little fun making up a ditty which she sang each time she passed their cage. It went like this:

> *Camels, Camels,*
> *Very silly mammels . . .*

The more she sang it, the more angry the camels became, and their cage rocked and swayed as they banged and hammered on the bars until Jacko made her stop teasing them, for he feared they would tear the very walls apart.

When Jacko and Fionuala had cleaned all the cages, Slow Joe sent them into the big tent to clean that too.

'Now we will see some of the wonderful acts again,' thought Fionuala in delight, but when they went into the tent it wasn't at all like the night before. No lights blazed down, no band played, and the whole tent looked quite grubby. The circus folk were dressed in tatty old jeans and tee shirts, and everyone seemed to be in a bad temper, and, in the worst temper of all, was Mr Hurry Harry. He stood in the ring cracking his whip and shouting at everyone.

The little girl who rode the beautiful white ponies sat eating an iced lolly which dripped all down her jumper, and when she rode round the ring she fell off, and cried so loudly that the ponies took fright and ran out of the tent. As for the clowns, they didn't tell even one joke or funny story, but stood in a corner being rude to everyone.

At last the sun set and Fionuala and Jacko's work for the day was finished.

'We must get away from this terrible circus,' she whispered, but no sooner were the words out of her mouth than Slow Joe appeared and took them back to their trailer. He put a strong lock on the door that even she couldn't open. They were so worn out after their day's work that they both went fast asleep.

11

The Restfields

Fionuala and Jacko fell into such a deep sleep that they didn't hear the noise and the music as the evening performance took place. They didn't hear the people laughing and shouting as they went home, and they didn't hear the camels moaning and groaning as they went to bed. They didn't even hear when the camels knocked and banged on their wall, and shouted some very nasty words.

When they did waken it was already morning and they heard angry voices raised in argument.

'There is nothing in that trailer,' they heard Mr Hurry Harry shout.

'Well, open it then and let me see for myself,' said another man's voice. 'I have had a complaint that you have been working an old donkey and a goat nearly to death.'

More angry words followed, but at last the door was opened and in flooded the morning sunshine. Outside stood Inspector John Reilly of the Irish Society for the Prevention of Cruelty to Animals. When he saw Jacko and Fionuala lying on the dirty straw, with no food and no water, he became very angry indeed.

'Mr Hurry Harry,' he said, 'you are a cruel man and I have a good mind to close down your circus and take away all your animals.'

'I didn't ask those old creatures to come and work

for me,' said Mr Hurry Harry sulkily. 'They just arrived and wanted a job.'

'I've had enough of your talk,' said Inspector Reilly as he led Fionuala and Jacko out of the trailer. Outside stood a landrover and a beautiful blue horse-box with ISPCA painted on its side in gold letters. Fionuala felt very proud as the Inspector led her and Jacko up the ramp, to a bright inside, where there was fresh hay and clean water all ready for them. By now many people had gathered to see what the fuss was about.

'Where are you taking them?' asked a little boy.

'To the Restfields,' answered the Inspector, 'for they are quite worn out with work.'

'Do you hear that?' whispered Fionuala. 'We're going to have a holiday!' and she felt very happy for she had never had a holiday before.

At that moment the camels passed.

'Good-bye,' Fionuala called out to them, and as

Inspector Reilly started up the landrover she sang at
the top of her voice:

> *Camels, Camels,*
> *Stupid big animals . . .*

It was well that the lovely blue horse-box was already
on its way, for the camels nearly went wild with rage
and it took six men all their strength to hold them.

'This is nice,' said Fionuala as they drove out of
Wicklow. There was a tiny window in the front of the
horse-box and she and Jacko watched the countryside
as it passed by. Inspector Reilly drove at a nice pace,
not too fast and not too slow, and he went carefully
round corners so that they wouldn't be bumped and
banged about.

Through the window they saw houses and shops,
tractors and cars. They saw a dog chasing a horse and
a horse chasing a cow. They saw fields full of sheep
and gardens full of flowers. They saw people walking
and people running and people standing still. But best
of all they saw a man pushing a pram and inside, as
happy as you please, was a little pig.

The journey to the Restfields took quite a long time
but Fionuala and Jacko enjoyed every minute of it.
She was humming happy tunes to herself as they sped
along.

ANIMAL RESTFIELDS said the notice at the gate. They
drove slowly past a large house and into a cobbled yard,
and as the Inspector helped them both out of the horse-
box, Mrs Reilly came hurrying along.

'What have you got there, John?' she called.

'Just you come and see, Peggy,' he replied. 'I've a

poor old donkey and a goat who've been worked nearly to death.'

Well, what a fuss Mrs Reilly made of Fionuala and Jacko, and how they enjoyed it. Then she and the Inspector took them down a little lane between high hedges, until they came to a gate. Inside the gate was the most beautiful green field they had ever seen. The sun shone down and all was peaceful. Butterflies flitted here and there, hovering over the wild flowers. In the field many horses and donkeys basked in the sunshine, and there was a little stream, where they could drink when they grew thirsty.

'Betsy,' called Inspector Reilly, and an old grey mare lifted her head and gave an answering whinny, as she trotted over to the gate.

'Look after this donkey and goat,' said the Inspector. 'Make them welcome,' and he opened the gate and led Jacko and Fionuala inside.

Inspector Reilly and his wife lent on the gate and watched as the horses and donkeys greeted Fionuala and Jacko.

'I can't understand it,' said Mrs. Reilly. 'That goat doesn't look at all as if she came from a bad home.'

'That's just what I was thinking.' answered the Inspector. 'In fact she looks a very well cared for goat indeed. Not like the poor old donkey who is quite worn out.'

'Did she tell you anything about herself when you rescued her from the circus?' asked his wife.

'Not a word,' said the Inspector. 'But she laughed and sang all the way here in the horse-box.'

The day passed happily for Fionuala and Jacko.

They grazed on the beautiful green grass and drank from the clear stream, and when the sun grew hot they sheltered under the tall trees.

As dusk fell Inspector Reilly walked amongst the animals and spoke to each one. When he left, closing the gate carefully behind him, the animals settled down for the night. A full moon rose, as with much rustling the night creatures came out. A fox walked by, his red coat gleaming in the moonlight, and a badger, nose to the ground, rooted around for insects. A flight of wild ducks arrived and, with much quacking, landed on the water of a little lake, while a hedgehog wandered under the trees. Many others came too, for they all knew they were safe in that lovely place.

As the animals rested they talked in low voices, and many tales were told. The old grey mare's life had been one of toil and much suffering. A little brown donkey told his story and his life, too, had been full of hardship.

'But now we can rest and have peace,' said a tiny pony, 'because Inspector John watches over us and we are safe.'

The next day Fionuala and Jacko again grazed on the rich green grass. As the sun rose high in the sky, she wandered down to the far end of the field where she could see down to the valley below. In the distance, there was a dark lake. She was already growing restless and had begun to think again of finding her family.

'Where is that lake?' she asked the old grey mare who was grazing nearby.

'That's Glendalough,' answered Betsy.

'Glendalough!' breathed Fionuala. A shiver of excitement ran through her, for she had arrived at the very place she was looking for.

'I must be on my way again,' she said to herself. 'At this very moment my family are probably down in that valley waiting for me.'

When she told Jacko she would be leaving, he became very upset.

'You can't leave,' he said. 'This is our home now.'

And when the other animals heard what she was planning, they too grew quite angry.

'What will we tell Inspector John when he finds you are gone?' said Betsy. 'He goes to all the trouble of rescuing you, and then you go off without even a thank-you. I call that very ill-mannered.'

'Yes, very ill-mannered,' chorused the animals.

'And ungrateful, too,' said Betsy.

'Very ungrateful,' replied the animals.

'I will send him a postcard,' said Fionuala.

'And where will you get that?' asked Betsy. 'Postcards cost money and you don't look to me as if you have any.'

'My family are very rich,' answered Fionuala haughtily. 'They are the Cool-Boys of Glendalough and have a large estate.'

'I never heard of them,' said Betsy. 'And I have lived here for years.'

Fionuala was growing quite angry with all this talk, but as she looked at the poor old animals her anger turned into sadness, for each one of them had led a hard life.

'Inspector John is a good kind man,' she said. 'And I am truly grateful to him for rescuing me from that terrible circus.'

'He is a saint,' said the tiny pony.

'And a gentleman,' said the animals.

'We would all be dead but for him' said Betsy.

'I do appreciate everything he has done for me,' explained Fionuala, 'and this is a beautiful place. But I *must* find my family. I will write a letter to Inspector John, if you will help me.' And she told the animals what she wanted them to do.

All day long Fionuala, Jacko, the horses and the donkeys searched the field and under the trees, and even in the stream, until at last they had gathered many stones which they put in a neat pile beside the gate.

As Inspector Reilly and his wife paid their last visit of the day to the Restfields, they noticed the pile of stones.

'How strange!' said the Inspector. 'I wonder where these came from?'

As the moon again rose in the sky, Fionuala set to work, and with the stones this is what she wrote:

Dear Inspector John:
Thank you for rescuing me from the circus and for bringing me to the Restfields. Now I must leave to visit my family in Glendalough.

Your grateful servant,
Fionuala Cool-Boy

It took her a long time to write the letter, for some of the stones were too round, some too small, and others too big, but at last she finished, and the animals gathered round to look.

'Very good,' they said, nodding their heads. 'Yes, very nice,' they all agreed.

'Will you not come with me, Jacko?' asked Fionuala. 'My family would make you very welcome.'

'No,' he replied. 'I'm a tired old fellow. I have had too many homes and this is where I want to spend the rest of my life, in peace and quietness.'

Fionuala had one more problem to solve before she could leave the Restfields, and it was a big one. She didn't know how to get out of the field.

Every evening when the Inspector said good-night to the animals, he put a strong padlock on the gate to keep them safe. Fionuala was a good jumper, but even she couldn't jump that gate, because it was a very high gate indeed. Round the field was a big wall and a thick spiky hedge, and though she walked round every inch of the field looking for even a tiny gap, there was just no way out.

She thought for a long while, and then she had an idea.

'I need a long stick,' she said, so once more the animals searched around. At last the very stick was found, not too thick and not too thin, and just the right length.

As the first note of bird song began, and as the first light of the morning came in the sky, Fionuala stood a little way off looking at the gate, holding the long stick the animals had found for her. She took a deep breath, and then she started to run. Faster and faster, nearer and nearer, until it seemed that she would run right into the big gate. But at the last moment she dug the long stick into the soft ground. She went sailing through the air as she vaulted right over the gate.

She stood in the grey morning and said 'good-bye'

to her friends. As she looked at Jacko she saw tears
in his eyes.

'I will visit you often,' she said. 'For I will be just
down the valley in Glendalough.'

'I hope you find your family,' said Jacko. 'If you
don't, perhaps you will come back here.'

'I'll find them all right,' said Fionuala. And with
a last wave she went quietly through the yard, past
the house, and down the road to Glendalough.

12

Glendalough

As Fionuala walked along the road to Glendalough her heart beat fast, for her search was nearly over. The road wound down, down, into the valley below and through the trees she caught glimpses of the dark lake she had seen from the Restfields. She thought of the surprise she would give her family and of the welcome she would get when they recognised her.

From time to time she stopped and scanned the landscape for a large house or maybe a castle.

'The Cool-Boys of Glendalough Castle,' she said to herself, and the more she thought about it the more sure she was that that must be where they lived.

She passed the Royal Hotel and stopped to look in through the windows. She could see soft armchairs and tables laid with knives and forks, and she longed to go inside for she was very hungry, but being a strong-minded goat she passed by. Round the corner she turned and there, right in front of her, was a flight of steps and an arched gateway.

'Surely this must be Glendalough Castle,' she said to herself, trotting up the steps and under the archway, but there wasn't a sign of a castle or even a large house anywhere.

'This is a strange place,' she thought as she wandered along the winding paths until she came to the Round Tower. Fionuala had never seen anything like it before,

and she stood and looked up, and up, until her head
began to spin, and even the Round Tower seemed to
be spinning too.

'What is it?' she asked herself as she looked at the
high slit windows and the dark stone walls, and then
she saw the guide-book. It was lying at her feet, as
if some kind person had left it there specially for her.

She picked it up and read it right through from cover
to cover, and from beginning to end. In fact she read
it twice, for she was a very careful goat and she didn't
want to miss a single word.

'Glendalough means the valley of two lakes,' the
guide-book told her. 'In the 6th century there was a
great city here of more than 3,000 people. Within the
city there were seven churches, cells for the monks,
halls for study, libraries, houses for composing and
copying manuscripts, workshops and factories,
surrounded by farms, fields and woods.

'The Round Tower is 31 metres tall. Being of such
a great height it made an ideal watch tower, and also
a safe place for both humans and treasures. The entry
door is 3 metres above the level of the ground and
when the city was attacked by the Vikings and the
Normans, the look-out rang the bell, and the monks
climbed up a rope-ladder and pulled it up after them.'

'The monks of old certainly knew what they were
doing,' thought Fionuala, 'for not even a goat could
climb those walls.'

She closed her eyes and tried hard to imagine what
it must have been like in Glendalough all those years
before, and as she was a very imaginative goat, she
could hear the bell in the Round Tower ringing, and

see the monks in their long habits hurrying along the pathways, carrying their treasures of beautiful books and gold and silver vessels to safety.

It was all so real in her mind with the sounds of battle drawing nearer and nearer, that she began to feel quite frightened. So she opened her eyes with a start, half fearing to see it all happening around her. But the paths were deserted and the only sound was the cawing of the rooks, as they wheeled and flew over the Round Tower and the tree tops.

'I wonder where I should go next?' she thought, and once more she looked in the guide-book.

'The Cathedral Church is dedicated to Saint Peter and Saint Paul,' she read, so off she set in search of it.

Now Fionuala had been to church, once. When she

was quite a young goat she had been taken to the Blessing of the Animals. She had loved the soft candlelight and the organ music and the choir singing, and she had been as good as gold and no trouble at all, until the Unfortunate Episode happened.

It hadn't been her fault, at least not to begin with. She has been standing quietly, not saying a word, not even when the donkey next to her brayed loud and long in her ear. She hadn't made a murmur either when a little dog sniffed at her heels, and she kept the same noble calm even when a big rude tabby cat spat right in her eye.

But then she saw the white mouse peeping out from the collar of a boy's coat. She liked mice, at least she liked the little brown field-mice who ran in and out of her stable, but this high-bred mouse was making the most awful faces, jeering and laughing at her, and she couldn't stand it for another minute.

'Look,' she whispered to the big rude tabby cat. 'Mousie ... mousie.'

With a loud 'mi-o-ow' the cat leaped out of his mistress's arms straight on to the boy's shoulders. The mouse jumped to the floor with the cat after him, and when the little dog saw the cat racing past, off he went too. After him rushed the donkey with the loud voice, and Fionuala followed the donkey.

Over the pews, up and down the aisles, round and round they all raced, with dogs barking, cocks crowing, children screaming, and every kind of noise imaginable in the background. It took quite some time before order was restored, but Fionuala was never taken to church again.

Along the path towards Glendalough Cathedral trotted Fionuala. As she drew near she felt sure she heard the organ playing and the choir singing, and she longed to see the beautiful candlelight again.

But to her great disappointment when she got there and went inside, there was no organ, and no choir, and no candles flickering. In fact there wasn't much of a church at all, for the roof was quite gone, with only the walls left.

'This is a very poor kind of a church,' said Fionuala to herself, and she looked at the guide-book again.

'Kevin's Kitchen,' she read, 'has a roof made of stone, with a small Round Tower inserted into it,' and she suddenly began to feel terribly hungry.

'I hope Kevin is a good cook,' she thought as she

hurried along sniffing the air, for she felt sure she could smell carrot soup and oatmeal biscuits and potato cakes. Down a little flight of steps she picked her way and as she drew near she thought she had never seen such a beautiful kitchen, with its stone walls and little tower in the roof.

In through the entrance — and what a shock she got! In fact she couldn't believe her eyes, for it wasn't a kitchen at all. Instead of a door there was an iron gate, shut tight, and as she looked through the bars, she could see a dark damp room, with not even a window, and bits of old stones lying on the floor. Not a sign of a shiny cooker, no brightly painted cupboards, no tables or chairs, and certainly NO food!

'I think I have had enough of this place,' thought Fionuala. 'One thing is certain; the Cool-Boys don't live here.'

Not far from Kevin's Kitchen was a swing gate. It was quite hard for her to open it because she had never seen a gate like it before, but after a few tries she managed it and she even had some fun swinging backwards and forwards. She crossed a little wooden bridge with a stream flowing underneath and dragon-flies, the colour of jewels, skimming over the surface.

Now the path ran between tall trees. Suddenly she caught sight of a lake. Two ducks were swimming on the water, quacking gently as they searched for food.

'Excuse me,' she said, 'I'm looking for the Cool-Boys of Glendalough. Can you please tell me where I will find them?'

'The Cool-Boys?' said one of the ducks. 'I don't think I have ever heard of them.'

'Of Glendalough Castle,' said Fionuala. 'Surely you know where that is?'

The ducks chatted together for a few minutes before answering. 'No,' they said, 'we have never heard of Glendalough Castle either.'

'Stupid creatures,' said Fionuala to herself. 'No wonder they're ducks. I'm *sure* I must be close by my ancestral home.'

The sun sparkled on the lake water and Fionuala sauntered along the pathway through a little wood until she saw a frog ahead.

'Good-morning,' she called. 'I'm looking for the Cool-Boys of Glendalough Castle. Can you please direct me there?'

The frog sat so deep in thought that she wondered if he had heard her.

'He must be deaf,' she said to herself, and she was just about to ask him again, when he spoke in a deep croaky voice.

'I can't say I have ever heard of them,' he said. 'But perhaps they live at the Upper Lake,' and he pointed through the trees. Then with a huge jump he disappeared into the reeds at the side of the lake.

Fionuala walked on and very soon she saw the lake. A cold wind ruffled its dark water and the only sound was the swish of little waves on the shore. No birds sang and no sun shone.

'This is a gloomy place,' she thought, as she looked towards the far shore where dark trees grew down to the water's edge. 'Not at all where I would expect to find my family.'

At that moment a stoat ran by, intent on his business.

He was a handsome fellow with a rich brown coat and a fine white shirt-front, and the tip of his tail was a beautiful black.

Fionuala didn't often associate with stoats for they were bad-tempered creatures, but she called out, 'Can you please tell me where Glendalough Castle is?'

'I can't tell you that,' answered the stoat. 'But I can tell you where St Kevin's Bed is. The tourists always want to know.'

'I saw his kitchen back there,' said Fionuala, 'and I must say I didn't think much of it.'

'Perhaps that's why he pushed his Missus into the lake,' answered the stoat. 'Maybe she couldn't cook,' and he gave a high-pitched laugh which sounded something like 'Tee-hee, tee-hee.'

'How terrible!' said Fionuala. 'Did he really do that?'

'So the legend goes,' answered the stoat. 'It's said that Kevin sometimes lived in a cave above the lake when he wanted a bit of peace and quiet like. Well this Kathleen kept following him there and annoying the life out of him. So one day in a fit of temper, he threw her right into the lake.'

'Did she drown?' asked Fionuala in horror.

'Well no one seems to be sure about that,' said the stoat. 'I think myself she didn't, but they say around here that on a dark night you can hear moaning and groaning coming from the lake. Do you know what I think?' said the stoat, lowering his voice and glancing at the dark water. 'I think it's the monster.'

'The *monster*,' said Fionuala, and her voice shook. 'Is there a *monster* here?' A shiver ran up and down her spine.

'Take your pick,' said the stoat. 'Monster or Kathleen. But there's something strange about this place and to tell the truth I don't come here too often myself,' and before she could say another word he was gone.

She sat and looked at the lake, and the more she looked at it the less she liked it.

'But I'm not turning back now,' she said to herself. 'Not having travelled all these miles to find my family.'

Drawn up on the shore was a rowing-boat, and as she looked at it she had an idea.

'If I could row out into the middle of the lake,' she thought, 'I might see Glendalough Castle, for it is probably just round the corner.'

Fionuala had never rowed a boat before, but that didn't stop her. She pushed it out into the water and climbed carefully in. She picked up the oars and started to row, but it wasn't as easy as she thought, and no matter how hard she rowed the boat just went round and round in circles. But Fionuala, as you know, was a persevering goat, and before long the boat stopped going round in circles, and she headed out towards the middle of the lake.

She was enjoying herself so much that she didn't look where she was going, and she nearly rowed into a large rock. That gave her quite a shock and she stopped rowing to recover.

Suddenly, looking up, she saw not *one* monster, but TWO. They were sitting on another rock only a few years away. They were black and shiny all over, with great goggly eyes and strange flipper feet.

Fionuala stared at the two monsters; then with a

scream of terror she stood up in the boat. It rocked wildly, throwing her over the side, and the cold dark water closed over her. She came to the surface, gasping and choking, and doing a strange goat paddle with much splashing, she made for the shore.

On the rock in the middle of the lake, the two frogmen looked at one another in amazement.

'Did you see what I saw?' asked one.

'Well,' said the other, 'I *think* I saw a goat rowing a boat, but you never can be sure of anything these days,' and they lowered themselves back into the lake to continue searching for buried treasure.

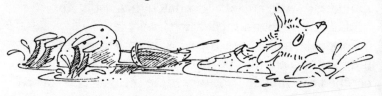

13

The Cool-Boys of Glendalough

When Fionuala reached the shore she took to her heels as if all the monsters in Ireland were after her. She ran and ran and then, leaping and jumping, she climbed higher and higher up the steep rocky path above the lake. It was only when she reached the highest point that she stopped. Down below not a movement now ruffled the dark waters of the lake.

Bit by bit her heart stopped thumping, and after a while she began to browse on the tender green shoots and succulent plants; she suddenly realised that she hadn't eaten all day.

She was so busy eating that she didn't see the cave until she was right beside it. It wasn't a very big cave and it smelt of damp things, but she was so tired that all she longed to do was sleep.

'I will be safe here,' she thought as she went into the cave. In a few minutes she was fast alseep.

She never knew how long she slept, but she wakened with a jump, for something was standing at the entrance to the cave. Something big and shaggy with horns on its head, and as she looked more shaggy figures appeared. Staring at her was a herd of large, wild goats.

The goats stood looking at Fionuala and Fionuala looked at those wild shaggy goats, as with pounding heart and teeth chattering with terror she backed into

the furthest corner of the cave, while outside the wind whined over the rocks in that lonely place.

Suddenly the first goat spoke and her voice echoed round the cave. *'Who dares to sleep here,'* she thundered as she advanced towards Fionuala.

'Have mercy on me,' bleated Fionuala, cringing against the damp wall of the cave, 'for I have travelled many miles from Sugarloaf Farm to find my family.'

'And what family is that?' asked the goat, peering at Fionuala though the gloom of the cave.

'The Cool-Boys of Glendalough,' whispered Fionuala.

Suddenly the cave was full of goats, all pushing and shoving, and Fionuala turned her face to the wall and closed her eyes as she awaited her fate.

Then something extraordinary happened. At first

she thought she must be dreaming, and then she though she must have died and gone to heaven and the angels were calling her, for she heard her name repeated over and over again.

She opened her eyes to find herself surrounded by goats, all smiling as they called out, 'Your search is over! You have found your family! Here we are!'

As Fionuala looked at those large, dirty goats, she grew faint with shock. There must be some mistake, she thought.

'My family are the Cool-Boys of Glendalough Castle,' she stammered.

'Oh, we don't use that old name any more,' answered the goats. 'We gave that up years ago.'

'If we called ourselves anything, it would be Cool-Girls,' giggled a young goat, and they all laughed in a most unladylike fashion.

'Where is the family estate of Glendalough Castle?' asked Fionuala shakily.

'Family estate, my eye,' said another goat. 'Don't talk such rot. Wild and free, that's us. We like the rain in our faces and the wind on our backs.'

'You mean you live out here on the mountainside?' asked Fionuala.

'That's just what we do,' answered the goats, and she felt weak with horror.

'You are very welcome,' said the old goat. 'I'm your Auntie Bridget and these are your cousins. This is Maureen and that's Carmel, and over there are Mary, and Fidelma, and Oonah, and Aoife, and Leila, and Grainne, and Niamh, and Cara, and the twins Ailish and Eilish, and little Patrick.'

Fionuala's head spun round and round as she looked
at her cousins, her dreams of a fine ancestral home
crumbling.

'Can you tell me about my mother and father?' she
asked weakly, 'for I can't remember them at all.'

'Wait until Kevin comes,' said Auntie Bridget. 'He'll
be here soon and will tell you all you want to know,
for he's very good on family matter.'

When Fionuala heard the name Kevin, her blood
ran cold, for she remembered what the stoat had told
her of the Kevin who had pushed Kathleen into the
lake, and she felt great fear.

'Has Kevin got a wife?' she asked nervously.

'Not him,' twittered Auntie Bridget. 'He's a real old
bachelor.'

'A girl friend perhaps?' said Fionuala.

'He's plenty of those,' answered Auntie Bridget. 'A
new one every week, for he gets rid of them fast.'

'How does he get rid of them?' asked Fionuala in
a weak voice.

'He just shoves them off,' said Auntie Bridget. 'And
here he is now ... Kevin,' she called, 'look who's here.
Little Nuala has come home.'

Into the cave stepped the largest, fiercest old goat
Fionuala had even seen. He was even larger than Big
Bill at Sugarloaf Farm, and his long, black, matted
coat nearly touched the ground. On his head were a
pair of magnificent horns, and from his chin hung a
dark beard. Fionuala shrank back against the wall of
the cave with fright.

'Well, well, well,' said Kevin as he peered short-
sightedly at her. 'It's little Nuala all right, and isn't

she the picture of her parents?'

And so, at long last, Fionuala learned her family history.

'Many years ago,' said Kevin, 'a lady goat of great beauty came to Glendalough and lived on a farm down in the valley. The moment your father laid eyes on her he fell in love, and he spent all his days mooning around like a love-sick cow. When at last that lady goat agreed to marry him his happiness was complete. He brought her up here to the mountainside, and in due course you were born, in this very cave.

'But the folks from the farm came for your mother and away down to the valley they took you both. Not long after that we heard you had gone to live at Sugarloaf Farm, and from that day we never heard another word about you.'

'What happened to my mother?' asked Fionuala.

'Well, it was like this,' said Kevin. 'Every week or two your father went down to the valley to get his

wife back, and I guess they got so fed up at the farm that they sent her back where she came from.'

'Where was that?' asked Fionuala.

'To Wexford,' answered Kevin. 'Your mother was a well-bred goat, very well-bred indeed. Saanen Princess of Wexford she was called.'

'Saanen *Princess* of Wexford,' said Fionuala, and her heart was filled with joy.

'She was a real lady,' said Auntie Bridget, 'and a great beauty, with a pure white coat and a long graceful neck. I believe her family came from Switzerland, but although she was high-born she was kind and gentle and we were indeed sorry when she left.'

'And what of my father?' asked Fionuala.

'After his wife went away,' said Kevin, 'he set off on his travels, here, there, and everywhere. The last we heard of him he was away down in County Kerry at Killorglin.

'Every year a great fair is held there called Puck Fair. They come from far and wide and there is great merriment, with singing and dancing and fun all day and night. When they grow tired of that the men go into the mountains to find a wild old puck. He must be brave and strong, a true Irish goat ... and didn't they choose your father some years back! Down to Killorglin they took him and there they crowned him King Finn!'

'My father a KING,' breathed Fionuala, and her heart nearly stopped beating she was so overcome.

Night was drawing in and a cold wind had risen, but inside the cave it was warm as the goats stood tightly packed together. Fionuala told them of her life on Sugarloaf Farm, and the goats told her of their life on the mountainside.

'We are glad to have you home,' said Auntie Bridget, 'for this is where you belong, with your own family.'

At last the goats slept, but Fionuala wakened time and again. She found the cave too stuffy, and as the goats stirred in their sleep she was knocked and banged and her feet stood on. Their long shaggy coats smelt strongly, and little Patrick cried and fretted in his dreams and had to be comforted.

As the early morning light crept into the cave, the goats wakened and one by one went outside and began to graze. Fionuala was the last to leave and when she did, a fine rain was falling and the air was cold.

Now goats, except wild ones, don't like cold or rain, so Fionuala was shivering as she followed the others who were now busy feeding a little way off. They were eating fast, tearing noisily at the short grass and moving on quickly, and Fionuala found it hard to keep up with them as she searched for food among the rocks and boulders.

'These goats are strange creatures,' she said to herself as she watched them pushing and shoving one another as they argued over the best places to feed.

Down below the lake was hidden from view by the driving rain, and as she peered through the mist Fionuala thought about the two monsters.

All day long she grazed with the goats on the mountainside and as she grew wetter and colder and more miserable, her thoughts turned to Sugarloaf Farm and her warm cosy stable.

'Perhaps it is time to go back there,' she thought.

As evening drew near the rain eased, but the goats grew restless.

'Something is coming,' said Kevin, ears alert, and they all became silent, listening.

'Is it a monster?' said Fionuala fearfully.

'Why do you ask such a strange question?' scolded Auntie Bridget, as little Patrick began to bleat and cry in alarm and the cousins giggled nervously.

Suddenly a gunshot rang out, and a man and a dog appeared over the mountain top looking for rabbits. The goats disappeared like the wind, all except Fionuala. For a few moments she stood and stared at the man, and then she too took to her heels.

Some hours later, when the goats returned, they found Fionuala all by herself, lonely and afraid.

'Why didn't you follow us?' asked Kevin.

'You ran too fast,' answered Fionuala.

'You were too slow,' said Auntie Bridget. 'In the wild you must be quick.'

As twilight fell, the goats returned to their cave. Fionuala had another sleepless night and as dawn broke she told the goats she had to leave them.

'Good-bye,' they called. 'Good-bye.'

'She is a nice wee thing,' said Kevin, 'but she would never make a wild goat.'

'Too delicate, just like her mother,' said Auntie Bridget, as over the brow of the mountain went the herd.

14

The Way Home

When Fionuala reached the foot of the mountain the sun was shining.

'Well,' she said to herself as she tripped along happily, 'not many goats have a King for a father, and a Princess for a mother,' and she felt very proud.

She came to the lower lake, and there, still swimming on the water, were the two ducks.

'Did you find your family?' they quacked when they saw her.

'Yes, thank you,' she answered.

'You didn't stay long,' they said.

'Long enough,' she said as she hurried down the path through the trees.

She crossed the little wooden bridge over the stream where dragon-flies skimmed the water, and she opened the swing gate and walked quickly through. She passed Kevin's Kitchen and the ruined church and the Round Tower without even a glance. Through the arched gateway, down the steps and past the Royal Hotel she trotted, and not once did she pause, not even to peer in through the windows.

As she came to the road which led to the Restfields she thought of Jacko. 'I would very much like to see him again,' she thought. 'He was a good friend,' but such was her eagerness to get home that she didn't stop but continued on to Laragh. 'I'll look him up another time,' she told herself.

'I wonder how Siobhan is?' she thought as she passed Laragh. 'I've a good mind to pay those Toggenburgs a visit,' but she hurried on until she came to Annamoe. Down the village street she went, past the pretty white cottages with the beautiful flowers, round the corner, and there looking over the wall was the little goat. Fionuala was glad to see he was still there and hadn't been put in a sack.

'I think I had better warn him about that man Pat,' she said to herself. 'He is a nice little fellow and I wouldn't like anything to happen to him.'

'Hi there, Missus,' called the little goat as she drew near. 'Have you had a nice holiday?'

'Very nice, thank you,' she answered. But when she told him of her fears about Pat, how he laughed.

'Oh no, Missus,' he said, 'you're got it all wrong. The only thing Pat puts into sacks are *oats*, not goats.'

Then Fionuala felt very foolish, and as she could see a lot of other little goats looking over the wall further down the road, all giggling, she decided to go another way rather than pass them.

A leafy lane wound out of the village, and this was the path she choose. Wild flowers grew in the hedgerows and insects buzzed by in the drowsy heat for the day had turned warm. On she travelled until she came near Lough Dan.

She began to feel very hungry, for it was many hours since she had eaten. She came to a gate which had been newly painted and she tried a lick of paint. She found an empty match-box and a cigarette packet and these too she gobbled up.

On she strolled, eating this and that, until suddenly she heard a strange noise in the distance. It was a roaring, zooming noise, and it was coming nearer every minute.

'What can it be?' wondered Fionuala. Then she thought of the two monsters of Glendalough, and the big mother pig who nearly squashed her flat, and the magic flute in her dreams, and she began to shiver and shake with fear.

'Perhaps they are *all* coming to get me,' she said to herself, and up the bank at the side of the road she jumped, and not a second too soon, for round the corner came a motor bike.

She had never seen a motor bike and she had no idea what it was, but she didn't like the look of it at all, so right over the bank she leaped and ran and ran until she came to a forest.

In among the trees it was cool and dark. Fionuala liked the wet earth and the soft moss under her feet. 'This is a nice place,' she thought as she wandered through the trees. The sun filtered down, mottling the ground with light and shade.

Suddenly she saw a very big shadow indeed, and that shadow was moving towards her. A large red animal with huge horns on his head stood right in her path, and worst of all he was looking straight at her.

'Excuse me,' said Fionuala in her most polite voice, 'but may I get past you, please?'

'The only way you'll get past me is back the way you've come,' answered the animal.

Fionuala didn't think that was a very nice way to speak, so she said in a loud voice, 'Dear me, you don't have to be so rude.'

As soon as she said that, the big red animal became very angry. Now Fionuala didn't know she was speaking to a red deer. He thought she was making fun of him, and if there is one thing a red deer can't stand, it is to be laughed at.

'None of your cheek,' he roared. 'Be off with you,' and he pawed the ground in rage.

She tried to run away, but she shook so much with fright that she couldn't put one foot in front of the other.

'Is there something wrong with your legs?' sneered the deer when he saw that she couldn't move.

Then Fionuala remembered the nasty judge at the Goat Show who had said such rude things about her legs. She stopped feeling frightened and she began to feel most annoyed.

'There's nothing wrong with *my* legs,' she answered, 'but perhaps there is something wrong with *yours*. You look rather staggery to me.'

She had hardly finished speaking when the deer flew into a terrible temper. You see this red deer was a father deer (called a stag) and he though Fionuala was being very insulting; and no stag can bear to be insulted.

'This is no place for me,' thought Fionuala, cowering away. 'I must get out of here.' She turned round to try and run for it, but what a horror met her eyes! For standing right behind her was another stag, and he was even bigger than the first one.

"Dear, dear!' said Fionuala, but she had the good sense to say it to herself, for if she had spoken out

loud she might not have lived to tell this tale!

At last she managed to get her legs to move and through the forest she raced. As she ran she could hear the two stags bellowing and roaring, and the crack of their horns as they met in battle.

She didn't stop running until she reached the edge of the forest and came to the mountains near Luggala. After a while, when her heart stopped pounding and her legs stopped shaking, she began to graze on the beautiful purple heather which covered the mountainside. She ate and ate, and the bees hummed by in the warm sunshine.

Suddenly Fionuala got the strangest feeling that someone was watching her, and she stopped eating and looked around. She looked here and there and everywhere, and then she saw Him — the biggest, whitest, most handsome billy-goat in the whole world. And she fell in love on the spot.

So Fionuala and the big, white, handsome billy-goat roamed the mountainside together, up and down the heather-covered slopes, until at last the sun began to set.

As it set, the rest of the goat herd appeared, and leading them was a fierce old nanny-goat. When she saw Fionuala with the big billy-goat, she was filled with jealous rage, and she chased her right down the mountainside.

'I think it is time for me to go home,' thought Fionuala as darkness fell. She came to Roundwood and went through the sleeping village, out on to Calary Bog. The night was still with a full moon, and the road stretched like a ribbon into the distance.

The night creatures were awake and about their

business. A fox crossed the road and disappeared silently into the bog, while a badger rooted around in the grass searching for grubs. She passed a family of hedgehogs, and a bat swooped low above her. There were strange noises in the hedgerows and an owl called from a wood nearby, but Fionuala was not afraid as she hurried on, longing to get home.

Not once during that moonlit night did she stop, until as dawn appeared, weary and cold, she came near Sugarloaf Mountain. As the sun rose, turning the mountain top pink, Fionuala drank deeply from an ice-cold stream, and after eating a little grass she fell fast asleep under a hawthorn hedge.

When she awoke she felt excited, for she knew she was nearly home, and she took to the road again.

As she came to the Long Hill of Kilmacanogue, a landrover passed her, pulling a lovely horse-box with ISPCA lettered in gold on the side, and who should be looking out but her old friend Jacko! The horse-box stopped and Fionuala ran up to it with joy.

How pleased Jacko was to see her. 'Where are you going?' he asked.

'Home,' answered Fionuala, 'to Sugarloaf Farm,' and she told him all about her family in Glendalough.

'Where are you going?' she asked when she had given him her news.

'I'm going to a lovely new home,' said Jacko, 'for I got tired of being in the Restfields with nothing to do.'

'Where is your new home?' asked Fionuala.

'Not far from here,' answered Jacko. 'It's called Enniskerry House.'

He pointed down into the valley below, and Fionuala saw the large house with the turrets and the towers and the beautiful gardens that she had seen from the top of Sugarloaf Mountain. It had been practically beside her all the time.

'I'll come and visit you,' she said, 'for you'll only be down the road.'

'That would be nice,' answered Jacko happily.

At that moment Inspector Reilly got out.

'Hello there, Fionuala,' he said. 'Are you well?'

'Very well, thank you,' she answered. 'I'm just on my way home.'

'Would you like a lift?' he asked. 'For we'll pass near your gate.'

So once more Fionuala climbed into the lovely horse-box beside Jacko, and Inspector Reilly drove carefully down the Long Hill until they came in sight of Sugarloaf Farm.

'Good-bye,' called Fionuala. 'Good-bye,' and she waved and waved until they disappeared from sight.

'I'll visit Jacko every week,' she told herself. 'What fun we'll have.'

15
Surprises

Fionuala was so busy thinking about Jacko's new home, that she was nearly at Sugarloaf Farm before she noticed the van. It was a battered old van and it stood right outside the farmyard gate. A strange man with a cap pulled well down over his eyes was walking through the gate and she didn't like the look of him one bit.

She crept quietly in after him and hid in the shadow of the wall to watch. He was doing some strange things. First he looked through the letter-box in the front door. Then he peered in through the sitting-room window, which she thought was a most impolite thing to do, and then he tried to open the window, which she knew wasn't the right thing to do at all. Next he walked over to the goat house and stood looking in through the open door.

Suddenly he did something very bad indeed, for from his pocket he took a packet of cigarettes and a box of matches, and he began to light the cigarette. Now everyone knows that it is dangerous to smoke near a stable or a goat house, for they are both full of straw.

Fionuala was a quick-thinking goat, and she didn't hesitate for a moment.

'FIRE,' she shouted at the top of her voice, and lowering her head she charged at the man. Just as he bent over to light his cigarette, she hit him a mighty blow. He flew through the air as if fired from a catapult, and he landed right in the middle of the dung heap.

'That will teach him,' thought Fionuala as she got ready to charge again.

'HELP,' screamed the man as he scrambled to his feet, and he ran for the gate with Fionuala thundering after him. He rushed out of the gate and, jumping into his old van, he drove off at top speed.

Fionuala felt very pleased with herself, and she looked around to see if anyone had seen how brave and clever she was, but there was no one in sight, not even a darting swallow, for the farmyard was quite empty.

'What a pity no one has seen me,' she thought, 'for I have saved the farm from burning.'

But someone had seen Fionuala. Lying on the stable roof, sunning himself, was the cat.

'So the old goat is back,' he said to himself. 'She gave that man a good hiding. I never thought she would be so brave.' And he looked down on her in admiration.

Now Fionuala felt very, very tired, so she turned into the goat house, lay down on her own bed, and with a contented sigh fell into a deep sleep.

The day passed and Fionuala slept. As evening approached the farmer and his wife returned and all the goats were brought in from the fields for the night; with them was Siobhan.

When they saw Fionuala fast asleep on her own bed, they crowded round her, all asking questions at once.

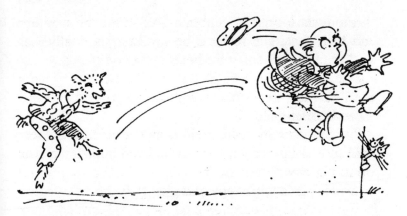

When the farmer saw her, he called his wife. 'Come quickly,' he said. 'Look who's here!'

'Can you beat it?' said his wife in astonishment. 'Where has she been?'

When at last the farmer and his wife went into the house and shut the front door, Fionuala told the goats of all the adventures she had and of her parents, Saanen Princess of Wexford and King Finn, and the goats were most impressed, all except Siobhan.

'If you are so high-born, why did you come back here?' she asked.

'I came back because I wanted to,' said Fionuala. 'And can I put the same question to you? Why did you come back? Would the Toggenburgs not keep you?'

To her amazement, big tears ran down Siobhan's face and fell with a plop on the goat house floor, as she began to sob quietly.

'I didn't like it there,' she sobbed. 'I couldn't understand a word they said, for they spoke only German.'

Fionuala looked at Siobhan and when she saw her sad little face, she realised how young she really was and she felt very sorry for her.

'Cheer up,' she whispered. 'I didn't really like my family either. Let's forget all about them, and you and I can be friends.'

So Siobhan stopped crying, and after a while she said in a sleepy voice, 'I really missed you, for it was no fun here without you.'

So Fionuala felt happy and glad to be home.

The next morning as the first grey streaks of dawn appeared in the sky, word spread round the farmyard of Fionuala's bravery and how she had saved the farm from burning. The cat just had to tell someone what he had seen, so he told the dogs. The dogs told the ducks and the ducks told the bees, and once the bees heard, the news spread like wildfire, and Fionuala became quite a hero.

'Fionuala is brave,' twittered the swallows as they flew here and there catching insects.

'Brave,' barked the dogs, and even the ducks agreed how brave she was.

All the goats now treated her with great respect, except Big Bill who refused to talk about her.

When the farmer and his wife heard what she had done, they made a great fuss of her.

'You know,' they said, 'Sugarloaf Farm was not the same without her. She is worth her weight in gold!'

Spring came and all the animals on the farm had their babies.

The cats had their kittens, the dogs had their puppies, and the ducks had fluffy yellow ducklings. One by one the goats had their kids, little brown baby goats, just like their father Big Bill.

Fionuala was the last goat of all to have her baby, but there he was one morning when the farmer opened the goat house door — a beautiful, pure white, baby goat.

'Bless my soul,' said the farmer as he looked in amazement at the little white kid. 'Where on earth did you get him from, Fionuala?'

Cool-Girl Fionuala of Glendalough, daughter of Saanen Princess of Wexford and King Finn, the bravest, cleverest, most adventurous goat in the whole world, said not a word, but smiled a secret smile as she tended her beautiful son.

The Adventures of Henry & Sam & Mr Fielding

Once upon a time there were three mice.
Three happy mice, but they all longed for
one thing and that was to have an Adventure.
So off they set on their travels — Henry the house-
mouse, Mr Fielding the field-mouse and Sam the
church-mouse — and what an exciting time they have!

After an adventurous journey, they spend a
pleasant summer in the land of milk and honey.
Then come the cruel days of winter. After a lucky
escape from Jack Frost and a dismal stay with a
dormouse, they meet Mr Fielding's long-lost Uncle
Bert. So they have a marvellous Christmas and
actually meet Santa Claus!

But Christmas makes them homesick and they
long to be home again. Their only hope is the wild
geese, about to fly north for the summer....

The Adventures of Henry & Sam & Mr Fielding
is a story of summer days, of woods and the
animals who live there, of the changing seasons,
of friendship, of misfortunes
bravely borne, and of the
pleasures of home.